SEVEN FOR A SECRET

SEVEN FOR A SECRET

ELIZABETH BEAR

SUBTERRANEAN PRESS 2009

First Edition

ISBN
978-1-59606-233-7

Subterranean Press
PO Box 190106
Burton, MI 48519

www.subterraneanpress.com

…it is clear that the Devil can make a Werewolf.

—Montague Summers,

The Werewolf in Lore and Legend, 1933

London
1938

1.

THEY SAY THE SECRET to getting away with murder is to tell no living soul. Well, the secret to getting away with lying is to believe with all your heart.

That goes for lying to yourself, even more so than lying to another.

The wampyr turned to watch two girls in the uniform of the Chancellor's Bund Englischer Mädel cross under one of London's new electric streetlamps, while motorcars rattled over the cobblestones and pedestrians gave the young collaborators a wider berth than strictly necessary. That, the wampyr thought. That was the core of the problem. He didn't believe his own lies anymore. He hadn't for decades. His artifices had grown shallow, without structure or craft.

He could no longer inhabit them. Not the way these girls, a golden-blonde and a paler blonde, inhabited their uniforms and the tissue of lies that constructed them.

The wampyr observed the girls sidelong, sound and motion and the taste of their warm, healthy bodies on the air. They laughed as if they had no idea that the epaulets on their grey wool shoulders were the color of blood. Jack would have been so outraged to see them. The wampyr thought he might have had to be physically restrained from a confrontation.

But then, that was the Jack of old, youthful and full of fire. He would be almost sixty now, if he had not been killed. If he had survived the intervening years, as well—those years that had so changed the wampyr. Perhaps they would also have changed Jack.

Why must he think of Jack now?

Because, he thought, the more golden of the two girls was slight and snub-nosed and looked younger than she was. Because, although she wore a revolver at her hip and the Iron Cross on her breast, though she was part of the conqueror's army, when her voice floated to him on the breeze, her words were in English and its accents were not German.

And if the first girl reminded him of Jack, the other one was as pale as Phoebe, but taller and broader-shouldered, her bearing limber and martial.

The wampyr thought the girls harbored a lot of courage, and not a little foolhardiness, to go out in London un-escorted. True, England had a long history of consuming its conquerors—in the end, the descendents of Celts and Saxons and Romans and French all became English after the fact. And true, the Germans had been in power eleven years, the younger generation was coming to maturity accepting foreign rule as the way of things. Also, the girls would be relatively safe here, on a public thoroughfare, with Schutzpolizei—the Schupo—visible every few blocks. But plenty who still inhabited London would not scruple over what became of two young collaborators, should they stray too far from a crowd.

The wampyr, himself, did not hold it against them. He was old enough to recognize that a seed could only grow where it was planted. Times changed, and those who would thrive must change with them.

The ways of London, however, did not change so much as all that. The girls led him through the tight medieval streets of ancient London-town, which still followed well-worn Roman pathways, familiar to the wampyr from the experience of centuries past. He altered his course through the pedestrians, past the bright glitter of shop windows in gray buildings, and came around to trail the girls at a distance. Phoebe and Abby Irene would not necessarily expect him home before dawn, even if they were wakeful, and it would do him no ill to see that the girls reached their destination in safety.

The act of following proved undemanding. Time-consuming, however, as the cadets seemed in no hurry to reach a destination. Instead they walked arm-in-arm, breaths streaming in the Christmas cold, footsteps falling in unison, laughing under their caps. They entered no stores, but seemed content to window-shop and giggle. Exactly as if they were not fifteen-year-old soldiers in the service of a conquering lord.

The crowds began to thin as the clocks struck ten; even in London, not much beyond pubs and gambling halls stayed open later. The wampyr dropped back, making more distance between himself and the girls. He was not terribly tall, and nondescript among London's men in his black city hat and greatcoat, but the habit of caution had kept him in the world a long time now and even distraction could not cause him to abandon it.

Now they huddled closer, using each other's bodies as a shield from the long night's chill. The golden one tugged the pale one's sleeve; they turned together down a winding way near the vast medieval Gothic cathedral of St. Paul's. The alley they chose kinked sharply. It would have been far too narrow for an automobile. The wampyr paused a moment to look up at the streaked spire of the ancient church rising above surrounding buildings like a white hen presiding over a mismatched clutch of chicks.

He shook his head, glanced over his shoulder to find himself unobserved, and slipped to the top of the crooked street and stole a glance down. The smell of the young women came clearly on the still cold air; they had stopped in the alley, and were filling the narrow space with scent—

their own, the light sweet scent of girls; the wool and gun oil and leather of their harness; their perfume—one wore violets, the other lilies; and another thing. A rank undertone of animal fur, like damp dog.

There were no streetlamps along this way, so the girls no doubt believed themselves concealed by darkness, and to any eyes but the wampyr's, they would have been. But the dark was his domain, his refuge, his office, and he saw through it as clearly as if through a thickness of black net. And he could hear them clearly, though they spoke in murmurs intended only for each other.

"…we can't get away with this forever," said the pale one. The wampyr heard every bit of worry in her voice as she said, "We could lose our positions."

The golden one was not concerned. The wampyr could find her scent clear on the cold wind, so he knew she was pleased and thrilled, running on excitement. She muffled her laughter with her hand and said, "We're *expensive*, Ruth. It's not so easy to replace a couple of sevens who are ready to graduate. Don't *worry* so much."

Her voice, a low ebullient whisper, told him before his eyes what he was about to witness. The girls did not embrace, because that would have rumpled their uniforms. But the pale one—Ruth—took the golden one's face between her gloved hands. The golden one's knee pressed up the hem of Ruth's skirt, her foot advanced for balance, her hands were on Ruth's upper arms, laid there lightly, with decorum.

There was no decorum to the kiss.

It was an invasion to observe them, but for a moment, the wampyr could not help but stare, mouth tight across his teeth, hands tightening on the silver head of his ebony cane. Envy, stark and simple, and after that a bright steel-tasting rush of worry for their sake. It was unwise, what they did. Brash and youthful and beautiful, and so sharply, perfectly unwise.

The wampyr heard the Schupo approaching long before the girls could have. He froze, elbows pressed to his ribs, and listened hard before he turned his head. The clip of the steel-toed boots on cobbles was unmistakable.

The wampyr could slip into the alley and be gone before the Schupo reached the corner. But then he would be leading the officer right down on the girls, like a fox leading the dogs upon the henhouse. And unlike that fox, the wampyr felt a sense of moral obligation.

He turned his back on the dark gap between buildings, leaned back against the red brick wall, and closed his eyes, the cane dangling from limp fingers. He didn't need to see. Close upon the Schupo's footsteps came his scent, tobacco and aftershave and the leather of his holster and his truncheon strap. Would anyone who smoked so much even be able to tell if the wampyr reeked of alcohol? Did it matter?

The footsteps closed, and stopped. „Wie heißen Sie?"

The wampyr opened his eyes, shaded them from the dazzle of the Schupo's electric torch, and shrugged. He had, he realized a little too late, forgotten what lie he was meant to be living.

In the alley, he heard the rustle of cloth, the girls' hesitant footsteps as they realized their peril and faded back, away, around the corner and into the dark dead end. They halted there, and the wampyr could imagine them huddled in the shadows, hearts racing like the hearts of hunted rabbits.

A coarse line was drawing itself between the officer's eyebrows. „Sind Sie krank?"

The wampyr held up his empty right hand, fingers extended, and made a gesture to his inside coat pocket. "My papers," he offered, in English.

The Schupo's squint relaxed marginally. He lowered the torch, away from the wampyr's eyes, but kept it trained on the center of his torso. Now his face was revealed; he was perhaps in his thirties, with a sandy moustache under the spiked cap.

"Yes," he said. His accent was better than the wampyr had expected. "Your papers, please."

Slowly, one-handed, the wampyr reached into his coat and produced them. They were a forgery, of course, but he was confident in them. What Lady Abigail Irene forged, no mere night watchman could put asunder. As he opened them for the Schupo, he glanced at his own name.

The papers read, *Dr James Chaisty Jr., M.D.*

"Doctor Chaisty," the officer said. "Have you been to visit a patient?"

"No, sir." Too easy to check a lie. "I visited a professional colleague. On the walk home, I was contemplating a tricky problem, and I seem to have lost track of time. I'm just on my way home now."

"It says here that you are the Garrett woman's personal physician."

The wampyr let himself smile, just a little. Abby Irene seemed as incapable of avoiding notoriety as a child of avoiding mud puddles. "Lady Abigail Irene is my employer."

"I read she'd come home to die. Now that it's safe for her to set foot in London again."

"With the Prussian government's kind permission, officer." It was still an effort to recollect that Germany had become Prussia again, even though that military transformation was the reason he had been able to bring Abby Irene back to London—and, in truth, the motivation behind their return.

"I don't trust revolutionaries." The Schupo shook his head, as if deciding to drop the subject before it turned into the sort of discussion that might require paperwork. "You've come a long way tonight, Doctor Chaisty. All on foot?"

Yes, the officer's English was quite good; he handled contractions with ease. Nearly as good as the German the wampyr was not admitting to. He would not have expected such fluency from a member of a force of occupation.

"All on foot," he admitted. He extended his hand for his papers. For a moment, the officer seemed hesitant to return them, but his face twisted slightly and he nodded. "All right. These are in order, and you may go. But Doctor Chaisty?"

"Yes, sir?" The wampyr tucked the documents away again.

"Be careful where you walk at night. This city isn't always safe for honest men."

As he watched the officer walk away, it occurred to the wampyr that Jack would have had something to say to that, also.

Ruth's heart raced with the kiss. In the cold dark, Adele's mouth was soft and warm. She smelled of lily-of-the-valley, a rich waxy sweetness at odds with Adele's coiffed hair and pressed uniform. Ruth wanted to press against her, unpin her dark-gold hair, feel the tumble of it across her fingers. Instead, there was only the resilience of chilled skin through her gloves, the tenderness of Adele's breath against her face.

"I wish we didn't have to go back," Ruth said, knowing as she said it that she was only mouthing nonsense.

"Silly," Adele said. "Where would we go? Where else would we have a chance to make our mark under the Chancellor's eye?"

Ruth didn't want to think about that, so she kissed Adele again, until Adele made a sound like a kitten, questioning and pleased, as soft and warm as her mouth. Their lips would chap, kissing like this in the cold, but Ruth didn't think it mattered. It was worth it to stand here in the street kissing her girl like the soldiers did.

But the soldiers didn't care if they got spotted. Nobody would interfere, or think less of them, though the girls who kissed Prussian soldiers sometimes got fruit or eggs thrown at them. And Ruth had to care, for her own sake, and for Adele's. And for their families. So when she heard the voices at the bottom of the street, the German one and the one that sounded English, Ruth darted back from Adele and held her at arm's length, pulling her farther into the shadows. "Schupo," she whispered, a hand across Adele's mouth. She could smell the men now, as the wind shifted. One wore damp wool and smelled of fennel sausage. The other smelled of cologne and something cold, and not very strongly of himself at all.

Adele, who was quick and brave, nodded and shook her head free. "Come with me," she murmured, her hand linking tight around Ruth's wrist. "There's not another way out, but the alley goes back."

"We'll be late," Ruth whispered. If they got stuck here long, they'd miss the last train. Curfew loomed suddenly, a formerly comfortable margin of safety shaved very fine.

Adele moved surely through the darkness, away from the voices, and Ruth followed her footstep on footstep. Her gloved hand rested on the cold butt of her revolver. Adele's hair glimmered in whatever faint light lost its way within the narrow confines of the alley, but her uniform vanished into the darkness. So long as they took care to walk quietly, the Schupo should never know they were there.

As Adele was leading, Ruth strained her ears to the conversation they left behind. Ruth's ears were very good and the men spoke as if they had no fear of being overheard, the Schupo crisp and Prussian, the other man pleasant and English. Ruth heard him say the name, and the Schupo reply with the name of his employer, and wondered.

What had he been doing by the mouth of the street? What had he done to interest the Schupo? Had he done it on purpose, to draw attention from Adele and herself?

Did that mean that he had been following them? And if he had been, why? And why had she not noticed him?

And why was it that she could barely now detect his scent, even with the looming walls to concentrate it?

They pressed themselves against the wall between the railings of two sunken yards, and Adele reached out to take Ruth's hand and squeeze it. It seemed like forever until the scents, the footsteps, and the voices moved away, while Ruth worried that cold sweat was freezing on her neck.

She worried all the way back to the barracks. Now, she and Adele walked quickly, heads down and collars turned up, hands shoved deep into their greatcoat pockets. As predicted, they missed the last train—they reached the underground station just as the porter was drawing the gates across the entrance. Ruth cursed under her breath, German words she was not supposed to know.

"We'll have to take a cab," Adele said. She sounded excited at the prospect; even the tiny maintenance Herr Professor allowed them was a fortune to Adele, the seventh daughter of a coal-miner.

A crescent moon had risen high enough to show between the brick and stone cliffs to either side. Ruth found herself glancing at it nervously, imagining she could feel it's streetlamp-washed rays on her face like Adele's fingers.

"We'll still be too late," Ruth said, but she still lunged out into the street, one hand raised, to hail a beetle-black taxi.

And she was right. Despite the cab, Adele put her key in the barracks door six minutes after curfew by the watch on Ruth's left wrist. Ruth forced herself not to rest her hand on her gun or slip a thumb underneath the holster strap to feel the outline of the wolf-fur belt she wore beneath it, prickly-silken, the heads of seven iron nails warm against her skin.

She knew who would be waiting for her and Adele inside, and she was pretty sure he knew they would be expecting to see him.

She could smell him through the door.

Lady Abigail Irene Garrett had not expected Sebastien to return before dawn, but she was nevertheless only nodding over a book in her chair before the gas fire when the key rattled in the lock. She awoke with a start, hands clenching on bentwood arms, her spine popping as her head jerked up. She paid for the reckless motion in the protests of muscles along the left side of her neck and back, but as the door swung open, she found the wheel rims with her palms and spun the left one back, the right forward.

She had grown so light that the chair spun in place without marking the old wood floor. Phoebe has taken up the carpets to make it easier for Abby Irene to move herself around. They had converted the back sitting room, which would have been Sebastien's once upon a time, into a bedroom so she never had to manage the stairs. He would not hear of hiring a nurse to baby-sit her, and after a fashion she was grateful for that. If someone must witness the humiliations of old age, at least it would be someone from whom she had no secrets.

She composed her hands on the arms of the chair. By the time the door opened and Sebastien's dark, narrow body stood framed against the night, she was certain she looked as if she had only just glanced up from the monograph she had been failing to read for several hours now.

He smiled tightly when he saw her, locked the door behind himself and shot the bolt, and dropped his key in a crystal bowl at the top of the hall. "Abby Irene," he said, and covered the distance like a blown leaf to kneel beside her chair.

He had not aged an instant, in the near-on forty years she'd known him. She should have envied him that immortality, she knew, but when she watched the expressions cross his face she felt only affection, and a tired sort of sorrow on his behalf. The pity had worn out years since, thank God. She did not wish to pity him.

She laid a papery touch on his hair, marveling at how her nails grew long and curved now that she did not work with her hands so often. When she had been younger, and trying to be beautiful, she would have paid a great deal for unchipped and elegant nails.

Sebastien said, "You are more beautiful than ever, my dear."

He might cast no reflection, but she could pick her own out of his glossy eyes. The skin drawn taut across her cheeks, the hollows under her eyes. Hair white and dry as feathers, carefully dressed away from her face.

"You are one hell of a strange wampyr," she answered, and leaned down to kiss his cool forehead. She had to steady herself against his shoulder to sit upright again, but he was a rock, unbending. "Where have you been? Did you find supper?"

She knew from his pallor and chill that he hadn't. There was more in that cold than the winter night.

He shook his head, and stood—not turning away, though he moved closer to the fire. "I am still building a court in London," he said. "I met Phoebe's young friend the surgeon. Perhaps he will serve. Perhaps he has more personality when he's at ease. But we parted ways after leaving the club." He shrugged. "There is no great hurry. Abby Irene—"

The tone of voice that only preceded a serious question, one requiring concentration and the application of intellect. She focused her wandering thoughts and said, "Yes, dear?"

"What sort of magic would make a young girl smell of wolfskin?"

"Wolfskin?" She didn't really need to repeat it for confirmation, and he knew that. His curt nod of response was however a little courtesy. "I seem to remember a vampire telling me once that there are no more werewolves."

"It was," he admitted, "my first thought as well. And as quickly dismissed. Also, what do you know about magic relating to sevens?"

She snorted. "What magic doesn't?"

He smiled, warming her. Ageless as ever, and still handsome. Every old woman should be so lucky. "Would you like me to fix you a drink?"

"Brandy," she said, and wheeled her chair closer to the fire again while he poured and brought it to her. "We've met with wolves before."

"The ghosts of them."

In France, in 1903. When they had encountered the revenants of a pack of wolves that had terrified medieval Paris, and young Jack Priest had met an abrupt ending.

She saw the implications of that memory reflected across Sebastien's face momentarily, before he stilled it.

Abby Irene cupped the snifter in her left hand. With her right, she idly rubbed the faded scarlet tattoo between her breasts. It itched a little, as it still sometimes did when she considered magic. Honoring the tradition among sorcerers, while the strength of her body waned the power of her magic had only waxed greater. "Tell me more about the girl."

"Girls. Two of them. Collaborationists, in the uniform of the Alliance for English Girls. Lovers."

"The Chancellor," Abby Irene said, tasting her brandy, "would be unlikely to approve. Are you certain?"

Sebastien smiled tautly. "They certainly kissed as if they were fond of one another. Anything beyond that is, of course, conjecture."

The alcohol stung her palate and sinuses pleasantly, but in truth, beyond that she could barely detect the flavor. Inevitably, all her senses were deserting her. "The Prussians have been known to engage in thaumaturgical experiment," she said, at last, unwillingly. "The sort of things most sorcerers would find unethical. But they consider very little beyond the pale when it comes to reclaiming their *Urheimat*—what they consider their rightful ancestral homeland."

"Ah." Sebastien bent before the fire, extending his hands to warm them. He would not feel a chill, but others might notice the cold of a December night in his hands. "Yes. I see."

Abby Irene folded her aching hands. "It is just possible," she said softly, "that this is the opportunity we have been waiting for."

Sebastien's thin mouth tensed. He had known before he spoke to her of it, she saw. And he was too much the gentleman, still, to point out that *we* in this case meant Abigail Irene Garrett, and the wampyr who indulged her insane schemes.

2.

WHEN RUTH OPENED THE door onto the dark-wood-paneled hallway, Herr Professor Schroeder had only just risen from the closest of a row of three intricate, high-backed Macintosh chairs. His briar still smoked on the stamped tin dish on a side table, a gold-rimmed coffee cup resting on a mismatched saucer beside it. He wore blue cloth slippers and striped pajamas under a diamond-quilted dressing gown.

„Miss Grell," he said, in German. „Miss Kneeland. I suppose you do not need me to tell you that you have endangered your privileges here."

If Ruth's name was first, did that mean she had been identified as the ringleader? If it would protect Adele, she'd accept the punishment. Though if it led Herr Professor to look too deeply into her background—

Well, that couldn't be helped now. She could only hope that it would seem less suspicious to brazen it out. „It is my fault we were delayed, Herr Professor Schroeder," Ruth answered, also in German. „I insisted we walk further, and misjudged the time it would take to return."

Adele tried to move up to Ruth's elbow, but Ruth sidestepped to stay in front of her and just managed not to wince when Adele stomped on her right heel.

Herr Professor folded his arms. „You realize that you have special privileges because you have special responsibilities, do you not? That those privileges and your permission to come and go are contingent upon your value to the Chancellor? You're very nearly graduates, ladies. You must acquit yourselves as responsible young adults, and not behave as children."

Carefully, Ruth nodded. From the corner of her eye, she could see the motion of Adele's cap as Adele mirrored her. „I am sorry, Herr Professor," Ruth said.

He still frowned at them over the bridge of his nose. „You are lucky seventh daughters don't grow on trees," he said, and let his hands fall to his sides, where he slid them into the patch pockets on his dressing gown. „Three demerits to each of you. Extra chores until you have expunged them to the satisfaction of Miss Krupps. And you are both restricted to the household until further notice."

Ruth licked her lips and discovered that she'd been correct. They were chapping. „Yes, Herr Professor," she said, as Adele echoed, „I understand, sir."

„Good," he said. „Now go up to your rooms. I shall inform Miss Krupps to expect you in the kitchens to help prepare breakfast."

Which meant rising before dawn. Short sleep was also a punishment.

„Yes, Herr Professor," Adele said, while Ruth was still considering that. Then Adele took Ruth's wrist in her chill strong hand and led her past Herr Professor Schroeder— who stepped aside to let them walk up the center of the hall unimpeded—down the long corridor, and up the stairs on tiptoe. They moved as silently as wolves past the open doors of bedrooms so they would not wake the other four girls in their class, who might already be in bed.

„That was close," Adele whispered. Ruth balanced their latchless door open a crack, as the rules demanded.

Ruth leaned back against the wall beside the armoire in relief and smiled at Adele through the harshness of the electric light. „Well, what *was* he going to do to us? Somebody just reminded me, it's not like sevens grow on trees."

When he was in the company of Abby Irene and Phoebe, the wampyr remembered to think of himself as Sebastien. Neither had ever quite surrendered the name they first knew him by, and in a moment of honesty he would admit he found it comforting. Mortals had the luxury of demanding permanence and having some slight chance of getting it. They did not need to acquire the skill of letting names, lovers, places slip through their fingers like hourglass sand. Sebastien knew of—though he did not subscribe to—an Oriental belief ancient by even his standards, which taught the same principals as a means of avoiding suffering. He wondered how many of his court would think it a chilly and nihilistic philosophy.

So whatever name graced his papers, he was Sebastien, at home. And would remain Sebastien a little while longer, at least to Abby Irene and Phoebe.

The former of those had indulged his curiosity about what it was that might make a human girl smell of wolf-hide. The library of their deep but narrow townhouse was carpeted, and so Sebastien parked Abby Irene's chair at one end of it and allowed her to bid him thither and yon, until the turned-leg table before her groaned with aged books.

After decades spent lightfooted on the continent, Abby Irene's library had been much reduced. But in returning to occupied London, she had found an unexpected legacy. The Crown Investigators had been disbanded, those sorcerers who had not fled the country detained, and the Enchancery replaced by a skeleton staff of Prussian Zaubererdetektive. Some might consider her a traitor to the crown—she had to admit, she numbered herself one such—but Abby Irene still had a friend or two in London, and a friend or two among those previously employed by the Crown's Own. Some of the Enchancery's rarer books had mysteriously disappeared in the early days of the Occupation. And through happenstance or by design, a significant number of those books had come into Abby Irene's possession over the intervening years.

Now, Sebastien triggered a latch on the book case that blunted one corner of the room and swung the entire piece of furniture open on concealed hinges, releasing the light scent of oil. There were more shelves within, concealed in what should have been wasted space created between the hypotenuse of the shelf and the angle of the wall. From within, he brought down an armload of tomes, many nearly as old as the printing press and created in an age when books were furniture, and nearly as large as couches.

The books were too well-kept and too carefully ensorcelled to reek of dust or mustiness, but Sebastien could clearly smell old leather, the dry protein of aged hide glue, the sharpness of ink. He was spared the acid reek of crumbling paper, because these books were printed on rag, and even after centuries their pages were still as white as starched shirts.

He stacked them on the desk and one by one began to lay them out, opening those which proved too heavy for Abby Irene's fragile old bones.

Abby Irene wore white cotton gloves and turned the pages with a slender glass rod. Sebastien's hands were devoid of the oils and salts that could damage ancient paper; he could handle the books directly.

It was a surfeit of riches, and Sebastien and Abby Irene were still huddled over the table when Phoebe came downstairs with the dawn. She paused at the library door and sniffed, leading Sebastien to wonder if Phoebe's merely human senses were fine enough to pick out the elements of the book-scent, or if she were merely surprised she could not smell must and mildew.

She was slight, and the silver in her hair did not stand out against the blonde. She adjusted her glasses on her nose and folded her arms, but after nigh on forty years, he could tell when her sternness was a mockery. "Sebastien," she said, arms folded over her blouse, "tell me you have not kept Abigail Irene from her rest all night and morning."

"Um." Sebastien glanced apologetically at Abby Irene, who was still bent over a book so thick that Sebastien could have slid three fingers under the arch of the spine. The back of one gloved hand rested against her forehead, the glass rod parting the strands of her snow-white hair. "Abby Irene?"

No response.

Sebastien cleared his throat again, then in a fit of help-lessness reached out and pushed fallen locks out of her eyes.

She started, and looked up. "I didn't hear you," she said. "I was concentrating. Good morning, Mrs. Smith."

Rather, she was growing deaf, and made it up by lip-reading. And Sebastien and Phoebe pretended they didn't notice. For a small kindness, her eyes were still sharp, though her reading glasses got heavier and heavier as the years went by.

Sebastien said, "Phoebe suggests that I am an unfit associate, having kept you up long past your bedtime."

Abby Irene pushed her chair back from the table, skinny, spotted wrists cording above the margin of the gloves. "I am eighty-eight years old," she said. "I shall sleep when I'm dead, Mrs. Smith. Or when the last Prussian boot tromps up the gangplank out of England."

Phoebe couldn't hide the twitch at the corner of her mouth. "As you say, Abigail Irene. Shall I roust the housekeeper, then, and see about tea and a soft-boiled egg?"

Mortals. Sebastien had never understood, exactly, how it happened, but somehow over the years Abby Irene and Phoebe had shifted from strained, formal rivalry to an equal formal and sharp-edged friendship that folded deep loyalty behind a mask of prickly dislike. The friendship had nothing to do with Sebastien, though it was his needs that had brought these two brilliant and unconventional women together, and he was pleased by the development. It suited him that these two oldest and most trusted members of his always-meager court had found an accommodation.

"That would be lovely," Abby Irene said. "Thank you, Mrs. Smith." While Phoebe still stood in the door, pressing down her smile, Abby Irene drew herself back up to the table and struggled to turn the heavy book. Phoebe withdrew. Abby Irene said, "Sebastien, look what I have found."

He touched Abby Irene's wrist lightly, so she would release the book to him, and turned it so it lay diagonally between them. "Werewolves," he said. "Except there are no werewolves. Anymore."

"That's not the first time you've said that, in just such a manner," she said. When he turned to catch her eye, he realized she'd been watching his face for a reaction, and wondered what she'd seen.

"It's not?"

"Paris. Where we met Doctor Tesla."

Where Jack died, but she wouldn't say that. Jack, who had been Phoebe's lover, and Sebastien's best-beloved… and so in the end, it had been Abby Irene who held them together until what was shattered began to set in its new configuration. Sebastien was terribly afraid that her courage then had left her with a sense that she had no right to remember Jack, to speak of him. As if by being strong, she had forfeited whatever sorrow she too might have felt.

Perhaps it had taken him decades. But he was beginning to understand Lady Abigail Irene Garrett. And she was not the sort to proclaim grief she did not feel entitled to.

"So I wondered"—her blue eyes squinted sharply over the bridge of her nose—"what experience you had had with werewolves to lead you to speak so definitively on the subject."

She was, Sebastien reminded himself, a criminal investigator. She needed no magic to pin a man on a stare. "That's pure conjecture," he said.

She smiled, satisfied. "You don't deny it."

"Deny nothing," he said. "Tell me what you found."

"Ways to build a werewolf. Other than contagion from the bite of another werewolf. Look. A wolf's-hide belt, enchanted and studded with iron nails—seven, or nine, or twenty-eight of them. Wearing a wolf's-hide into battle, as some Vikings were said to do. Born under a caul. One could be cursed by the gods, if one were an ancient Greek—"

"Lycaon, who gave his name to the breed."

"Just so." She pushed her shoulders back, as if wishing she could straighten her spine properly. "Sleeping outside under a full moon was said to provoke the transformation, though if that were the case, one would expect a commonality of werewolves. Drinking water from a wolf's footprint. There were liniments as well, and I've found recipes for some. Eating ergot or henbane…."

"Eating ergot might make your *neighbors* seem to be werewolves, in any case. Henbane was used to flavor pilsner before the Germans outlawed herbs other than hops in beer. That might also make for a lot of werewolves."

"Another way to become a werewolf is…" and here Abby Irene smiled her sunken smile "…by being born the seventh son."

"Really?"

"Really." She tapped the page lightly with her glass rod.

"What about the seventh daughter?"

"That is supposed to make you a witch," said the sorceress. "Personally, I've never found a correlation. But sevens are magical in all sorts of ways."

"The seven sayings of Christ in his passion," Sebastien offered, as Phoebe returned to the room. Behind her trailed the housekeeper, Mrs. Moyer, bearing a tray with one three-minute egg, a selection of toast points, and a steaming teapot.

"Going religious, are we?" Phoebe asked.

Abby Irene caught the comment this time. "Don't put that tray by the books," she said. Mrs. Moyer was already clearing off a side table. Her expression never so much as twitched.

"Magically significant sevens," Sebastien explained.

"Seven virtues, seven sins," said Abby Irene. "Seven continents and seven seas. It is a number of great ritual importance."

Phoebe pulled out a chair and sat, folding her hands neatly across her lap. "Seven fingers and toes and eye-pupils of Cuchulainn, the Irish hero."

"Trust you to come up with something obscure."

Phoebe winked. "Not if you're Irish. And if you are Jewish, God rested on the seventh day, and one takes seven days of mourning. There are seven branches of the menorah and seven archangels." Was it a thought of Jack that brought the frown across her face, Sebastien wondered, or was he casting his own emotions on her?

Abby Irene, pretending obliviousness, continued, "The murder of Cain will be avenged by God seven times."

Sebastien nodded. "Seven is the number of God the world over. Hinduism offers seven chakras, and seven sages. In Islam, there are seven heavens and earth, seven doors to heaven, and seven fires in hell." It was the religion of his mortal youth, though in a millennia past it had changed as much as Christianity. He would not say that, though. Not only were they uncomfortable with change, but the mortals hated to be reminded that their ancient traditions were often no deeper than a century—or less.

As if age and custom had aught to do with value.

He drew a breath to continue speaking—he only needed breath for that—and paused instead. They could sit and list sacred numbers all morning, and Abby Irene's egg was getting cold. "Abby Irene," he said, making sure he had her attention before he spoke further. "How do you plan to use this information to bring down the occupation?"

The old sorceress gave him a bent, ironic smile. "Magic," she said. "Sebastien, would you bring me over to my breakfast, please?"

Phoebe cleared her throat. "So if we have got were-wolves, what are we going to do about it?"

Abby Irene rolled her shoulders. "What would you do with a cadre of invincible fighters, Mrs. Smith? If you were the Chancellor?"

"Send them to the Russian front," Phoebe said promptly. And then she stopped herself and said, "No. I'd keep a few for myself, and send the rest to the Russian front."

Abby Irene's lips drew taut over her toothless jaws. "Just so, Mrs. Smith. Just so."

"The first liniment, then, is composed of the fat of young children seethed in a brazen vessel until it becomes thick and slab, and then scummed. With this are mixed *eleoselinum,* hemlock; *aconitum,* aconite; *frondes populeae,* poplar leaves; and *fuligo,* soot."

—Montague Summers, *The Werewolf in Lore and Legend,* 1933

They secured their revolvers, braided their hair, and got into their nightgowns. Adele slipped into Ruth's narrow bed as soon as the lights were out. Despite the trouble they were already in, Ruth slid an arm around Adele's waist and spooned against her back, pushing her nose against the nape of Adele's neck. She still smelled of lilies and hairspray, and under her nightgown Ruth could feel the outline of the wolf-skin belt. It wasn't really too dangerous, sleeping together fully clothed; neither the housekeeper nor Herr Professor was likely to find it suspicious. Most of the girls did it; they had all grown up post-War destitute in big families, sharing beds and body heat. They wouldn't be here if they hadn't. They all found it strange to sleep alone.

Ruth wondered, though, if any of the other volunteers were in love. You weren't supposed to fall in love with other girls. But Adele loved her too—had kissed her first, in an act of desperation, one night when Ruth found her hopelessly crying and unable to explain.

And now they cuddled together, breathing in unison, and whatever the future brought, they would face it together. Just knowing that made uncertainty easier to bear. Ruth knew that the Bund was supposed to instill confidence and loyalty to Prussia in English girls. It worked on some—Adele and Ruth had both lived here since they were twelve years old, and sometimes it was hard even for Ruth to remember that there were other ways of thinking—and with some it was hard to tell. Everyone mouthed the rhetoric.

Which of them really believed in her soul what the Prussians said was anybody's guess. Ruth presumed most of the girls didn't have reasons as good as hers to distrust what the tutors told them. But Ruth's grandmother had died in the camps. Her grandfather, who had barely escaped Prussia with his life to join his son in England before the invasion, had spoken in great detail of starvation, of men and women and children rounded up and shipped like cattle in boxcars to workhouses and to murder factories.

So she held on to that, to the memory of her Zayde's toes nipped-off from frostbite, and it was easier to remember that everything Herr Professor Schroeder told them about the master race and their special place in the world was horrible lies. It helped her smile to him, and lie right back with conviction.

Whatever Herr Professor Schroeder thought about Ruth being the ringleader, it was Adele who made sure they were up and dressed, faces and hands cold-water scrubbed and their hair combed wet and braided tightly back before sunrise. So when the crisp knock came on their door, Ruth could simply open it and step through, ready for duty. Rebecca, the maid who had come to awaken them, was too well-disciplined to betray either surprise or satisfaction at their preparedness. It was, Ruth thought, a skill she should also cultivate.

„Miss Krupps is expecting you," Rebecca said. She was no older than Ruth, but a servant rather than a student—brown-haired and weak-chinned, with the watery eyes and transparent complexion of a true Englishwoman. She raised a flickering taper in a copper holder beside her face. There was no economy in using electric lights for one servant to walk up the back stairs and collect two disgraced girls from their dormitory.

„Thank you," Adele answered. „Are you to show us down?"

„As you wish, Miss."

Single file, they descended the servant's stair, another mark of disapproval.

Miss Krupps was the housekeeper, and Ruth thought her as tidy and complete as a cat. She even looked rather like a cat, green-eyed under her soft steel-gray bun, with a tendency to tuck away stray tendrils of hair as if grooming her whiskers and ears. She was soft-spoken and considerate and Ruth also thought no one with the slightest trace of common sense ever would care to see her anything but soft-spoken and considerate. Some people wore their authority with a booming voice and a swagger. And some wore it as if it were a veil—weightless, seemingly inconsequential, but always present.

Miss Krupps was wearing that authority as she stood waiting, aprons in hand, until Rebecca delivered Adele and Ruth unto her. „You've left your pistols in your room," she said, disapproving.

Ruth, tying off her apron, said, „Yes, Miss Krupps. We thought they would only be in the way."

Miss Krupps frowned. „Tomorrow, you'll wear them. What is your duty?"

Ruth and Adele answered in unison, „It is our duty at all times to be ready to defend the Homeland and the Chancellor, Miss Krupps."

Sternly, the housekeeper nodded. „Today, you may take extra marksmanship practice over the lunch hour to correct the oversight."

Adele frowned at Ruth. Ruth, with an effort, managed not to return the grimace. Short sleep and no luncheon, then, in addition to the extra work. „Yes, Miss Krupps," Ruth said, while Adele echoed her a half-beat behind.

Adele added, „We're sorry, Miss Krupps," and somehow managed to sound as if she meant it, though Miss Krupps studied them each by turn, gaze intent under an unpersuaded brow.

Finally, she nodded and turned away. „You won't permit it to happen again. You'll find scrub brushes, paring knives,

and potatoes on the drain board. Please dice the potatoes for
Bauernfrüstück, and let me know when they are done so I
can have you start on the onions."

Ruth tried to keep her expression ladylike and serene, as
Herr Professor preferred, but she was afraid she glowered at
Miss Krupps' back for a moment too long. Adele saw the
glare; Rut knew because Adele tugged Ruth's elbow and
moved her towards the big sink full of cold water, and a pile
of potatoes suitable for serving a hearty breakfast to twenty-
three—two adults, and twenty-one students ranged in age
from ten to sixteen.

Abby Irene didn't realize she'd nodded off over her
breakfast until she felt Sebastien's cool hand cupped behind
her neck. When she opened her eyes again, she saw her own
hands resting on either side of the breakfast tray and the
cracked-open egg with a half-eaten toast point resting beside it, all distorted through the reading glasses slipping
down her nose.

"Phoebe's right," Sebastien said. "I've abused you shame-
fully. To bed, Abby Irene!"

"I'm not a child," she said grumpily, painfully aware of
her own querulousness and how ridiculous it was to protest
adult competence while still lifting her chin from her chest.
Old age might as well be childhood, for all the capability

and self-determination it stole. Her neck ached abominably, as did her crabbed hands. She closed her hands on the table edge when he would have rolled her away, knotting her jaw stubbornly. "I'm going to eat my breakfast, *if* you are quite finished with wronging the ancientry."

His sigh stirred the hairs at the nape of her neck. She was supposed to be too old to feel a thrill at his nearness, but a shiver ran up across her scalp and around her throat nonetheless.

"Ancientry, are you now? I am not two-and-twenty, Abigail Irene. Nor are you a shepherdess." He kissed her scalp, cool lips, the weight of his hands on her shoulders.

"Oh, but I am," she said. She fumbled up the toast point. It was cold, but that didn't matter. "And see, I have failed the sheep." She would have made a broad gesture, taking in all of London, but she needed both hands to steady the egg cup and manage the toast. "And the wolves have come in among them."

Sebastien, admitting defeat, gave her shoulders a soft squeeze before he stepped away. He came around her and poured off her cold tea into a potted palm. There was yet sunlight, though clouds promised to seal the sky by lunchtime, so he made sure not to come too near the window, though the back of the house still lay in morning shadow and the conservatory roof beyond gave the protection of shade.

He refilled the cup and set it by her hand, for which she rewarded him with a smile. He leaned a hip against the edge of the table, his shoulders against the wall, and folded his arms as he glanced down at her.

She was not used to seeing him defensive. She looked down, at the toast and jellied egg, and this time managed to get the damned thing into her mouth.

As she gummed it, Sebastien said, "Do you really think the Prussians would...."

She swallowed toast, washed it down with tea, and said, "Ulfhethinn."

Sebastien blinked at her. "I don't know that word."

She sighed and pushed her spectacles up her nose, careful of potentially eggy fingers. There was nothing sadder than an old woman with food on her face. "Sebastien. Tell me you didn't know any Vikings in the ninth century."

He snorted laughter. "I walked East, when I walked. And I have forgotten most of that. So what are Ulfhethinn, mi corazón?"

"What is an Ulfhethinn, you mean. Plural Ulfhethnar. The wolf-hided ones. Do you know what a Berserk is?"

"Bear-shirt," he said, nodding. "There was a werewolf equivalent?"

"History is divided as to whether they were shape changers or merely possessed of a wolf-spirit—"

"Merely," he interrupted mildly.

She covered her yawn with the toast-free hand and smiled. "As you say. But the Prussians have something of a fetish for Teutonic imagery. Which is to say Norse imagery, to a fair approximation."

"It's endearing when you lecture."

She set the last corner of toast down on the plate. "Do you wish the answer, or not?"

Abby Irene had observed that wampyr learned quickly not to nibble their lips, the way a human might, but from the expression on Sebastien's face he was wishing for something thoughtful to do with his mouth. "I am avoiding the topic," he admitted.

"I noticed." She had had as much cold egg and toast as she could stomach. It didn't take much to surfeit her these days. "According to Snorri Sturluson and Saxo Grammaticus, berserkers served as the hired guards of kings. They were renowned for their ferocity and dauntlessness, and those who would not serve lords were dreaded mightily. Some took the wolf as their patron. Those dressed in wolfskins and dined on smoking wolf-blood. It was said weapons blunted themselves on their hides, that no arrow could pierce their hearts, that they would fight without armor and tear the throats from the mightiest warriors with their teeth."

If he were human, she thought his face might pale. As it was, he unfolded his hands and rubbed them across his cheeks, eyes, and eventually—vehemently—through his hair. "I remember."

"And yet you've never heard of an Ulfhethinn." Maturity brought some wisdom. She kept the archness from her voice when she said it, and was actually rather proud of her level tone.

"Never." When he looked at her between the columns of his forearms, she saw the rumple at the corners of his eyes and knew it was the closest he could come to a smile just then. "But I have met my share of werewolves, of the moon-cursed sort who pass their sickness on a bite, like hydrophobia. And you should know, Abby Irene, that they are terrible."

"The stories endure—"

"The stories do not begin to do them justice." He glanced over his shoulder, while Abby Irene did him the dignity of not presuming he was checking for Phoebe, but rather making a point of not shocking the servants. "Do you recollect the Beast of Paris?"

She had not heard him speak on it since Jack's death. By his drawn expression, he would have preferred not to speak on it now. She reached out and laid the back of her left hand against his hip where it touched the small table, and thought by the twist of his mouth that he drew some strength from the contact.

A dying sorcerer comforting a wampyr by the laying on of hands. In all the wide world, would wonders never cease?

When his hand fell to his side, it fell over hers and clasped it, as if by accident. Would it be easier for him when she was gone, and so was Phoebe, and all of them who had known Jack passed from his existence, into the realm of memories where Sebastien so reluctantly delved?

It is the secret to his survival.

If she could forget everything she had lost—Richard, Henry, two homelands, her life's work—would she become immortal, too? Sorcerers lived a long time, by habit and preference, but now at the end of her life, she rather thought ninety years or so would suit her. If she could set right some of the things that had not developed as she would have preferred them.

There are always unintended consequences. Something Sebastien had tried to explain to her and Jack both, so many years before.

She did not think she wanted to live forever. Not now that King Phillip was dead, and Prince Henry with him, and all of England's royal family that remained was in exile with the new Phillip, the old Phillip's son. In New Amsterdam, for bitter irony.

She supposed it was a kind of ironic justice, that her own treachery had created the safe haven that now sheltered her dead lover's nephew, England's King-in-Exile.

She swallowed all that and said, "How could I forget?"

He grimaced. "Then imagine if you will the twin of it for destructiveness, a wolf which may be harmed by no mortal weapon. With the size and cunning of a man and a lust for human flesh that will not be assuaged. Have you ever seen a flock of sheep when the wolves have run among them?"

She shook her head and squeezed his cold, firm hand. "I've never lived anywhere where the wolves were anything but a memory. I've seen what a dog can do to a rabbit hutch, however. And I've seen human carnage."

"There is no slaughter like the slaughter we wreak on our own," he said. He placed her hand gently on the table and stepped away. Walking around her, he took the handles of her chair again. This time she allowed it. He finished, dripping irony, "If I may be permitted for the moment to include myself in the human race."

You only do so when the comparison is unflattering. The wheels bumped on the edge of the carpet as he brought her into the hall. Her bedroom was on the other side, also in the back of the house. Once it had been a sitting room, and if Abby Irene were young again, she would have converted it into a laboratory.

She said, "The irony of a wampyr in awed discussion of the destruction wrought by another supernatural creature is not lost on me, you know."

"I didn't think it would be," Sebastien said. In her room, he shut the door, and turned to open her wardrobe. "Will you let me help you put your nightgown on, Abby Irene?"

Outside, because this was London, Abby Irene heard the rain begin. She had missed the sound in America. Not that it didn't rain there, certainly. But it did not often rain the way it rained in England. "Fill the basin so I can wash my face? If I have my cane, I can walk that far."

The blue flannel gown over his arm, he silently folded aside her lap robe, handed her the thick briar walking stick, and—once she had wrapped her hands around it—helped lift her to her feet. She set her spectacles down and steadied herself against the side of the basin while he poured water from the ewer that had grown too heavy for her to lift, and dabbed a flannel in it. As he handed her the cloth she said, "I think you are speaking from personal experience, Sebastien."

He began to unbutton her cardigan—his own knitting—from the bottom while she scrubbed at her face, and when she had set the cloth down he slid it off her shoulders and hung it on the bedpost, in case she should be cold. "I have hunted werewolves in my time."

She had been with Sebastien nearly half her life. She knew the ghosts buried in that simple statement as if he had spoken them aloud. As he helped her raise her arms to slide the nightgown over her head, she decided it would not be a kindness to suggest that she understood that he had not merely hunted them, but perhaps also had been acquainted with one or two.

It wasn't as if she really needed to hear his answer.

3.

BY THE TIME SEBASTIEN had called Mrs. Moyer to draw the curtains on a rainy English morning and so darken Abby Irene's bedroom, the old sorceress was already dozing. Sebastien, like so many of the Blood, had the trick when he so pleased of almost-vanishing. There was no magic in it, just the silence of a weightless presence: the unbeating heart, the lungs that stirred no breath. Now, he allowed himself to fade into the shadows of the bedroom, watching Mrs. Moyer adjust the drapes and Abby Irene drift into sleep.

She lay composed upon the pillow, arms crossed over a breast that rose and fell in patient rhythm. It seemed wrong to him that there was no small dog curled at the foot of the bed, chin resting on Abby Irene's ankle, eying him mistrustfully. Since he'd known her, she'd kept a succession of nondescript dust-mops with prickle-sharp teeth. Upon the demise of the previous one, she had declared it "unfair" to adopt a replacement, and had refused to be swayed.

She seemed somehow incomplete to Sebastien without a terrier. But it was her decision, and one he must respect.

Mrs. Moyer walked out past him and shut the door without a sideways glance. She hadn't noticed him, and must have assumed he'd slipped out while she was busy at the window. Because he was alone, Sebastien allowed himself to smile. If he were just a little less material, he would pass through husk and into spectre.

He didn't think it would be so bad, if that was what became of him. And it might be; he had already grown into the oldest creature he had ever heard of. And he knew he grew stranger, more disconnected, stronger and yet more adrift, with every passing decade. They flitted by like weeks—he could recall, dimly, when a decade had seemed like a significant stretch of time, but now it was nothing, fluff blown from the hand. A mortal's lifetime, be it fifteen years or fifty, was over almost before he felt he'd begun to know them.

But there was Abby Irene, eyelashes fluttering on her crepe-paper cheek, lovely as a faded flower, lying alone in her narrow white bed. And perhaps the wampyr could still learn from the example of a mortal courtier.

Or perhaps for his kind, letting go was simply another path to burn.

Maybe that was where all roads led in the end.

She did not awaken when he slipped from the room.

Back in the library, Sebastien found Phoebe sorting books and frowning. He slipped up behind and kissed her nape beneath the gray-spiked spiral of her bun. She jumped, but not too high, and by the time she came down off her toes again she chuckled. It sounded strained, but her voice stayed soft and welcoming. "Werewolves, Sebastien?"

"Prussians," he replied, as if that answered everything.

She grimaced. "What *would* delight them more than a cadre of lycanthrope shock troops, hearkening back to the pure Teutonic roots of the Germanic Empire? What could be more glorious proof of their divine right of conquest?"

"Nothing," he spat, jamming his hands into his pockets.

She might be able to maintain a voice of sweet reason. The bitterness in his made up for it. She drew back, studying his face until he couldn't bear to think what she might see there, and turned away. He needed to move. He knew very well that she followed him down the hall to the front parlor, farther from Abby Irene's bedroom door. In truth, he welcomed her persistence.

The curtains in the front window stood wide, the shade thrown up. He leaned a hand on either side of the sash, and stared out at the rain. The glass cast back no image of himself nor ever would, but after a moment, he saw from Phoebe's reflection that she had come up behind him. She touched his shoulder. For a moment, he could not think what he should do to react, and so he did nothing at all.

"What are we doing here, Sebastien?"

"Letting Abby Irene die in London. Didn't you read the papers?"

"Law of unintended consequences," she said. "We did what we felt we had to do. As much as you like to assume responsibility, you are not personally liable for the fall of British Empire, and neither is Abby Irene."

"Jack would not have approved of the Prussians. And neither does Abby Irene." He shrugged, which made him able to feel the weight and warmth of her hand on his shoulder. He should feed soon, he thought, though his appetite no longer troubled him except in extremes of need or injury. "Human memory is too short. Every generation must fight the same wars over again as if they were new ones."

She smirked. "Perhaps we need wampyr to run the world for us."

"Oh, yes," he said archly. "That would no doubt provoke innovation. We have had some positive effect before, Phoebe. We freed the colonies."

"We helped, at least." Phoebe stepped close enough that Sebastien could feel her heat through the fine cloth of her blouse. Fashions for women were much improved by the retirement of the whalebone corset, he thought, and certainly the ladies of his acquaintance seemed much relieved by modern undergarments. Progress occurred. Just not always in the manner one would prefer.

She said, "Having been instrumental in freeing the colonies—if we were, if it would not have happened just as inevitably without us—does not make you responsible for

England and France exhausting themselves in war, Amédée Gosselin."

An even older name than Sebastien, and one just as abandoned. She used it now for a reason, as a reminder. No matter how the romances are written in later centuries, revolution was never the work of one man. If Germany, France, and New England could each be democratized to such variance of effect, what chance was there of working any kind of prediction at all? Well, none, and he had long known it. "No," he said. "But it does make it seem possible that perhaps we could prove of some utility in overthrowing another conqueror, does it not?"

"And if there are consequences?"

He stepped back from the window, so her arm bent from the elbow until their shoulders touched. "Then there are consequences."

Her fingers squeezed. In the glass, he saw her hand tighten on nothing, then drop to her side. "You *are* the Scarlet Pimpernel."

It was perfect and unexpected, the sharpness that he admired. "Amédée Gosselin," he corrected. He turned to her, and in his dressing gown he swept a mocking bow. "At your service."

She should have laughed. Instead, she watched with a frown, touched her lips with one finger, and said reluctantly, "You're like a stone sometimes."

He straightened and nodded, venturing a smile. "From the inside, too."

England's ceaseless rain meant freedom for Sebastien, though that freedom did not come without risk. He asked Mrs. Moyer to have Jason bring the car around, swathed himself in rain cape and overcoat and hat, chose an umbrella from the stand beside the door, and stepped out into the rain.

Umbrellas blossomed like a mourning garland along the pavement. As the Mercedes purred up to the curb, its black hide glossy in the rain, Sebastien added his own bloom to the bouquet and stepped from under the door-awning and down the puddled walk. Jason trotted around the car to hold the door, and Sebastien ducked down to enter. Strange to step down into a vehicle rather than up to one, but he had grown accustomed to stranger things. Before allowing Jason to close the door, he folded the umbrella behind him and gave it a useless shake, sending droplets flying. The rain hammered down with enough authority that it grew wet again before it was dry.

As Jason slid into the front seat and behind the wheel, adjusting his cap and the mirrors, Sebastien thought he would like to learn to manipulate this arcane machine with its levers and lights and dials, the rumbling motor under its long domed bonnet. Perhaps he was not quite ready for the knacker yet, if gleaming technology could still enthrall. He remembered with clarity the first time he had seen a water-clock, a horse-drawn coach, a steam locomotive. It took mortals to invent such things. Wampyr, in growing their experience, became too attached to it.

Yes, he thought. He would learn to drive the car.

"Where to, Dr. Chaisty?" Jason was playing the role. He, like Mrs. Moyer, was perfectly aware of Sebastien's nature. There was no hiding such things from servants, and so the wise wampyr hired staff who were already well-informed of the needs and preferences of his kind. There were social organizations that made such things possible.

Those organizations had other justifications as well. Sebastien purposed to visit one now.

"My club, please. The underground one."

In the dark, he would have walked the short three miles, but there was too much risk in changeable weather. So instead he sat back and folded his arms over his chest while Jason navigated expertly through crowded, spring-rattling streets. A car was still a great luxury in the Americas, but in England and on the Continent, the Prussian Empire's resources made petrol cheap and plentiful. So the Mercedes was far from the only vehicle on the road, which was also clogged with pedestrians—most of them brandishing still more black umbrellas—carriages, lorries, cabs, traps, and the last of the morning's delivery wagons, drawn by steaming, miserable-wet yellow Suffolk Punches and slate-colored Percherons.

The drive required only twenty minutes, a significant improvement upon walking. "Shall I wait, sir?" Jason asked.

"Please. I may be a little while."

"I shall take the opportunity to enrich myself with literature, sir." Jason turned, to grin over his shoulder, distracting Sebastien with the tendoned arch of his throat and the sweet-salt tang of blood under his flesh. It was time, past time, for Sebastien to refresh himself.

And yet the reluctance grew. He would see to it today. Once he was done in the club. Jason or Phoebe should be able to oblige him; it had not been too recent a thing for either.

It was up to him—the wampyr—to behave responsibly, to distribute his attentions where they would comprise no undue burden. Because the court could not always be trusted to make those decisions for themselves.

Jason opened the curb-side door and Sebastien stepped out, pausing to murmur in Jason's ear as he passed. "Tonight?"

Jason's face split with a grin. "Very good, sir," he said, shutting the door crisply. "I'll just bring the car around out of the thoroughfare and wait for the doorman, then."

Courtesy of cloak and umbrella, the wampyr remained almost entirely dry up the long walk to the door, which swung open in anticipation to receive him. He stepped through, handed his accoutrements and a tip to the doorman, and breathed a quiet sigh as the silence of the club's interior settled over him.

Here there was no smell of cooking food, of cigarettes, of perfumes or whiskey as one might find in any human-frequented establishment. There were courtiers in attendance, of course—one could hardly expect one of the blood to play porter on the dayshift—but out of deference to their employers, the humans who worked in an underground club indulged their needs and vices elsewhere.

The wampyr entered a calm softly-lit room, the windows obscured with tortoiseshell mosaics that would admit light but not the burning sun. The curtains hung over them were drawn back, golden-brown translucence giving the effect of soft summer light rather than the gray winter beyond. The legs of deep chairs and low tables dented opulent rugs, and behind the bookcases the walls were dressed in figured velvet. This was merely the visitor's room, the antechamber, and the wampyr passed through and down a hall between sets of doors, to find the arched entryway at the end.

In a gentleman's club, this would be the smoking room, with its tall windows open on the back garden to permit light and air within. In this place, the exterior wall was ringed with a broad verandah with louvered sides, through which Sebastien could make out glimpses of rain-beaten green. Though it was December, the windows and the louvers stood open, and the scent of rain and grass and bruised earth filled the chamber.

There was another manner in which an underground club was different from a gentleman's club. As he entered, someone rose to greet him, and her skirts swung as she turned. The style was slightly archaic but flattering, long enough to brush the arches of her heeled boots, and she wore a prim nipped-waist jacket over a white linen blouse. Her hair hung in scarlet corkscrews on either side of her stone-white face, which was round and pleasant and remarkable chiefly for its air of extreme youth, an air reinforced by fine, arched brows and a childish upturned nose. She was adorable, cherubic, as she had always been.

"Paolo," she said, breaking into a wide and startled grin that showcased the gap in her teeth. "Though I suppose you cannot be Paolo anymore, can you?"

She still had a faint Scottish accent. And as for him, he remembered the name more easily this time. "James," he said. "James Chaisty. And you—?"

"Alice, still. Alice Marjorie. No one remembers a woman for twenty years." She winked, and came to embrace him. "You look like the light would shine through you, James."

"I feel it, too." He wondered what she felt when she put her arms around him. She was sculpted, flesh over bone, firm and cool. He imagined he might crackle like papier-mâché. "I've gotten old."

She stepped back. "You are the eldest, now. Or the eldest I have heard of. After Evie…"

"It was a long time ago," he said, though forty years was not so long as that. "You can say she burned."

She tipped her hand and cocked her head to one side, a birdlike gesture he knew well. "How is it, getting old? I hear it's made you political."

He shrugged. "Perhaps someday I'll have a sensible answer. Are you here merely as a traveler?"

A delicate query, delicately phrased. Alice thought about it. "Are you asking if I've grown political too?"

"A pretty euphemism."

"I've seen enough border wars to last me a millennium, James." She evidenced no hesitation over the name, as if she had known him by it for a lifetime. But her face had always been revealing, the hazel eyes transparent to her emotions.

He already suspected her answer, and he took no pains to conceal that suspicion from her. "Then you do support the Chancellor?"

Her laugh almost knocked him backwards. "Damn you. You know I don't. And I'd hazard there's not a chance you support him either."

"See?" He took her arm to lead her to a pair of chairs by the open window, where the clean scent of rain could wash over them, and he seated her there with a little ceremony. "I always said you were clever. You've come to talk to Ian, then."

She nodded. "I've come to see how I can help."

That inflow of cold air concealed any scent, but Sebastien heard the creak of boards under the hall rug, and by the quirk of Alice's head, she heard it too.

"Speak of the devil," she said, as the ancient and stolid Ian MacGregor turned the corner into the doorway and paused there, arms folded under his gray patriarch's beard, tweed jacket rumpled over the sleeves of his sweater and gnarled horny fingers poking from fingerless mitts.

"Oh," he said. "No devil, lass. Just an old troublemaker. It's been a long time since I saw you two together on my couch."

"Uncommon circumstances," Alice said. "Hello, Mr. MacGregor. You're missed in Edinburgh."

"Edinburgh is missed in me." MacGregor came to them, one foot dragging, and settled in a third chair opposite. "But I'm needed in London. What brings you out by daylight, Dr. Chaisty?"

Sebastien glanced at Alice. "Forgive me...."

"No trust even for old times' sake?" But she smiled, already standing. "That's wise of you."

As she stood, MacGregor would have risen again if she had not pressed him into the chair with a hand against his shoulder. "*Your* knees are not immortal," she said kindly. "Stay sat, old man."

He turned, anyway, and watched her from the room. Then he turned back to Sebastien. "You're a damned fool."

Sebastien smiled thinly. "That is not a revelation. I've brought you something that may be important."

MacGregor looked up. "Well, don't draw out the suspense, Doctor."

"Wolves," Sebastien said. "I think—and Lady Abigail Irene thinks, which should impress you more—that the Prussians are trying to recreate the Ulfhethnar shock troops of yore."

"By God," MacGregor said, eyes all but disappearing into his squint. "Those Huns. What an excitable lot of cunts."

When Miss Krupps released Ruth and Adele from duty in the kitchen, there was barely time to make their morning lessons. After morning lessons followed the missed lunch, and an hour in the basement range, firing their revolvers against targets tacked to a wall built of damp sandbags. Beatrice Jane Small smuggled them bread from lunch wrapped in her handkerchief, which they wolfed while scrubbing the gunpowder residue from their fingers before Deportment and then German Conversation—though their entire day was German Conversation, as all classes were taught in it. Neither Adele nor Ruth of them had a chance to rest or share more than a hurried word until the hour before dinner.

They were meant to bathe and dress, but it was all Ruth could do to fall into the yellow chintz chair beside their window and let her head drop back upon the upholstery. „I die!" she cried, and plastered the back of her hand to her forehead like a talking-picture heroine.

Adele toed out of her shoes (a demerit, if Miss Krupps saw the scuffmarks) and flopped over backwards on her bed, waving her striped stockings in the air. Her uniform skirt rucked up her thighs, but Ruth was too tired even to properly appreciate the view. She closed her eyes and turned her feigning palm over to cover them.

Adele said—in English, five demerits—"Let's never get caught again."

That was good enough for a laugh. But not quite good enough to uncover her eyes. „We must dress. Or it will be more of the same tomorrow. And there is practice after dinner. Don't count on any more sleep than we got last night."

Adele groaned, heartfelt. She said, „At least it's nearly graduation. And then, glorious service to a United Aryan Homeland!"

Ruth winced behind her hand, hoping Adele thought it was just exhaustion. When she found the strength to raise her head, she saw that Adele had pulled one foot up like an inverted bug and was pressing her thumbs to the sole. „Dress shoes. And we are meant to believe in a just and loving God."

„God may be just and loving." Ruth pushed herself up on the arms of the chair and wobbled to Adele's bed, where she made the springs creak as she flopped down. „But the Chancellor rules by blood and steel. Come on, give me that."

Adele barely protested as Ruth pulled her foot into her lap and took over the work of massaging the arch. After a moment, she relaxed into it and purred. „I will not survive dinner."

„You will." Ruth patted Adele's ankle and stood. „Now come on. Braid my hair for me first, and I'll brush off your uniform while you do yours."

Bathed and dressed, Abby Irene spent the afternoon in the front parlor with Phoebe, adrift again on a sea of books. The two women mumbled over pages in a range of languages, at intervals pushing passages under one another's noses for confirmation or a second opinion. The research led them to speculations, yes. But those deductions came at the expense of encroaching apprehension.

When Sebastien returned around tea-time, deductions and apprehension had solidified into a hypothesis. Abby Irene watched through the archway to the hall as Mrs. Moyer met him upon his entrance. Rain dripped from his weather gear and the brim of his hat until she divested him of that armor. Beyond the front windows, all she could glimpse of pedestrians passing beneath the street lamps was bobbing black fabric stretched over articulated armatures, obese raindrops obliterating themselves in cascades of spray. The street beyond the pavement ran an inch deep with rain-embossed water, each complex of ripples imbricate over the others until the interference pattern broke into chop and chaos. It became impossible to pick one event from among thousands.

War was like that. And history. And countries. Anyone might draw clear margins around a thing, set it apart, treat is as discrete and contained inside its borders. But the map was not the territory, and as soon as you got close to one of those arbitrary lines, you found all the things they cut across. Cause and effect were a spiderweb, where every choice and every reaction ran into every other one, and you could not tug one without tearing the next.

Abby Irene rested her fingertips on the carved leather cover of a closed book and called out, "You were gone a long while."

Sebastien finished unwinding his cloak and passed it off to Mrs. Moyer. "I had a long and edifying conversation with Mr. MacGregor, and then I had to atone for rudeness to an old friend of the blood. Then, despite the rain, it seemed provident to wait for darkness when darkness was so near. Have you ladies settled on what you'd like for tea?"

Abby Irene made a left-handed, irritable gesture. "Whatever it is, I shan't taste it. What did Mr. MacGregor say?"

Sebastien came across the threshold and settled like a windblown leaf into the chair just inside. It was a narrow-legged Queen Anne, embroidered yellow chrysanthemums on pale Chinese brocade and dark wood carved to elegant curves. Abby Irene kept it—and kept it beside the door—

because it was extraordinarily uncomfortable. The wampyr never seemed to notice.

"He'll contact the human resistance with your information," Sebastien said. "He's obtained a list of the girls in the Bund. There are twenty-one. Six in the oldest group, the rest younger. We will suggest local cells be instructed to contact their families and learn what they can about the young women—"

The wampyr stopped abruptly, hands resting on his knees as he leaned forward. "Hmm."

"Sebastien?" Phoebe asked, perhaps a little too much the ingénue for a woman of her age.

He smiled, an expression not calculated to express happiness. "I infer from your expressions that you've uncovered some further evidence of catastrophe in my absence. Out with it, my loves."

Phoebe glanced at Abby Irene, who shrugged. So Phoebe said, "Why would a Prussian militia recruit English girls? Collaborators? Why trust them?"

"If we still like Abby Irene's theory, many royal guards are traditionally mercenary organizations," Sebastien said. "And yet, I gather that's not what you're driving at."

Abby Irene gummed her lower lip while Phoebe explained. "I think you'll find, when that information comes from the families, that these girls do not have a great deal of choice in their assignment. But if they're allowed to walk the streets without supervision, then they are granted privileges as a means of controlling them and winning them over. Which means that whatever means of control their commanders have over them is not physical."

"The families?"

Phoebe nodded. "What else?"

"That seems a very fragile strand by which to rope someone you hope to forge into a bulletproof killing machine. But if they are taking the girls at a young age—"

"Eleven or younger," Phoebe said.

Sebastien winced. "Early enough to remake their philosophies, I imagine."

Abby Irene stroked her hands over the book before her. She had marked the relevant page in her leatherbound book with a ribbon. It took her both hands to lift it, and before she could try to extend it Phoebe had lurched out of her chair and was beside her, lifting it off her hands. Abby Irene would have growled, but she was out of breath, and she didn't recover it until after Phoebe had delivered the book into Sebastien's hands and returned to her own chair. He found the ribbon—really, Abby Irene could have marked the page with nothing more than the scent of her hand, and he would have found it, but it was nice to observe the social prevarications—and parted the covers.

As he bent to read, Abby Irene said, "Binding oaths. A Wyrd."

"That's forbidden magic," Sebastien said, his gaze traveling down the center of the page. "It's mind control. Outlawed in every civilized nation." He shook his head.

"Because the Chancellor is so concerned with laws, except the ones he has a hand in writing. Laws for deportation, detention, eugenics, medical experimentation, final solutions to invented problems—"

"Phoebe," Sebastien said, raising his gaze. "I am sympathetic to your disgust, and, as it happens, in complete agreement."

She'd been building up to a fine tear and now she stopped, hands on her hips, and breathed out sharply under a glower. She shook her head and let her arms go limp, palms pressed to her thighs. "I'm sorry," she said. "I'm sorry. But you understand—"

"Yes," he said, and closed the book upon his finger. "Abby Irene—"

Abby Irene lifted her chin, knowing she resembled a hound on a scent. "You think I'd mind-control those children? Sebastien. But what if we could promise to spirit their families to safety? Do you think that might make a difference in their loyalties?"

Sebastien tossed his head like a restive horse. "There's another solution." He turned away from Abby Irene and Phoebe, as if uncomfortable with the pronouncement he was about to make. He stood, and went to the window. Beyond it, the night hovered. Abby Irene knew what he saw, invisible rain drumming on the planished street, the dimpled ripples broadening.

"The suspense," Phoebe said dryly, "is killing us."

The book cradled against his chest, he turned away from the rain. "It was you who called me the Scarlet Pimpernel, mi corazón. We'll go and get them."

Abby Irene heard her own intake of breath and saw Phoebe's spine stiffen. Phoebe said, "And if the Prussians are using their families to control them?"

He folded his other arm over the book, as if it were some wholly inadequate piece of armor. "We smuggle out Jews."

Abby Irene felt a chill settle into her belly. "Sebastien," she said. "I think you may be unrealistically optimistic about your chances of convincing these young women to come away."

He lifted his chin, disapproval creasing his forehead. "And also, you want to use them as a weapon against the Chancellor. Which you cannot, if we rescue them."

"Wartime rules," Abby Irene said, and made herself meet his eyes. "What's a couple dozen lives, Sebastien, measured against millions?"

4.

THE AFTERNOON DRILL ENDED with forty-five minutes of catechism in the rights and duties of Prussian officers and Prussian women, which Ruth had memorized to the point of dreaming it. Which was a lucky thing, because she could barely keep her eyes open for the duration of the lesson. The question-and-response seemed endless, chants like a litany, and she knew she would hear it echoing in her head for hours afterwards.

By dinnertime, it appeared all was forgiven. Or expunged in Ruth and Adele's hard work and suffering. They took their places among the other girls without remark, though Ruth caught the littlest ones whispering at the bottom of the table. Their own agemates—Beatrice Small, Joan Mapes, Katherine Ressler, and Jessamyn Johnson—simply kept their eyes lowered and their hands folded, waiting for Herr Professor to take his place at the head of the table. It was Jessamyn's turn to sit in the hostess's place at the foot of the table, for which Ruth was grateful. She did not think that she could manage to support a spirited conversation among the youngest students today.

It was all Ruth's willpower not to fall on the bread and butter like a starving wolf while they waited, but poor table courtesy was another way to earn demerits, so—even though her stomach was rumbling loudly enough that Beatrice shot her a sidelong smile—she folded her hands in the lap of her dress and bowed her head while Herr Professor said Grace. When the bread was passed, she broke it into dainty pieces dabbed with butter, eating in small ladylike bites.

This was part of the discipline, too. Ruth felt Herr Professor's gaze upon her every time she lowered her eyes to her plate, and so extended herself in courtesy to the girls sitting across from and beside her. Manners, decorum, strength, courage, loyalty.

The virtues of a mastiff dog.

She owed it to her family—to the world—to excel. Adele would understand, when it was done. Adele would forgive her.

Practice occasioned another costume change. Pleated knee-length skirts and tennis shoes were at least quick to slip into, and Adele was the best in the class at braiding hair. When she did it, the process might bring tears to sting Ruth's eyes, but the braid stayed put.

Ruth smoothed her blouse over her wolfskin in the mirror, frowning critically at her reflection. She needed larger shirts. Adele came up beside her, pushing her braid aside to kiss the side of her neck, and Ruth slipped an arm around her waist and tugged her close. She felt the prickle of Adele's wolfskin through her blouse, too, and leaned her head on Adele's shoulder.

Adele kissed her ear. „Do you think anyone will do it tonight?"

Ruth shrugged, and let her arm slide free as she turned to the door. „There's only one way to find out, isn't there?"

Downstairs in the long high-walled garden, the class shivered under a striped awning that kept off the rain but not the chill. Ruth and Adele were not the last to come down, though, and even Katherine, who was, still arrived four minutes early. Herr Professor would be punctual, which meant the girls had a few moments to straighten their shoulders and adjust one another's collars and hairpins, and wonder what might be under the canvas tarpaulins covering a single long table set against the wall. They would not lift the edge of the drop cloth, however. Not where Herr Professor might see.

By the time the sliding door from the headmaster's quarters opened and Herr Professor appeared framed against the light, his uniform cap tugged low and his greatcoat collar turned up against the rain, the girls had lined up side by side in two rows. It pleased him when they were ready for him.

Neither rain nor cold seemed to affect him as he descended the steps from his patio. He carried a swagger stick under one arm. His glossy boots clicked decisively on stone as he strode along the walk through thumping raindrops.

Ruth would have given anything to cross her arms over her chest. The wind iced through her thin cotton blouse. Her whole body was goose pimples and shivers, and the only way to keep her teeth from chattering was to clench her jaw. Judging by what similar tautness did to Beatrice's face, perhaps it made Ruth look stern.

She knew this was to toughen them, but it didn't make her hate it any less. Still, she kept her chin up as Herr Professor's gaze skimmed across her. He spoke in German; whatever he said, Ruth let the words wash over her. The response was ritual, always the same: Protokoll, Dekor, Kraft, Mut, Treue! She had to unlock her jaw to chant in unison with the other girls. Protokoll, Dekor, Kraft, Mut, Treue! Protokoll, Dekor, Kraft, Mut, Treue!

Over and over, until the words had no more meaning than the ones Herr Professor bellowed. Ruth did not want the words to have meaning. She did not want to believe them.

She did not want to believe them in German. In English, they were her life.

Or, she thought calmly, her death, more likely. But that was okay.

It would be worth it.

She was still clutching that thought to her breast as if it were warm when Herr Professor held up a hand to interrupt the call and response. With the others, Ruth fell silent. She pressed her arms against her sides as if to trap some ghost of warmth—a useless gesture—and tried not to shiver too loudly as she waited.

Herr Professor scanned the girls, inspecting each one's uniform and deportment with a gimlet eye. Adele and Jessamyn, he each tapped with his swagger stick, but lightly, to improve their posture. Ruth would like to do the same to him, but she thought she kept the fantasy from illuminating her expression.

Finished, Herr Professor set his shoulders and said, „You know you have been chosen for a great purpose. A great destiny. You have each risen to a tremendous challenge, and each proved yourselves worthy of the glorious Prussian Empire.

„But now you must rise to an even greater and more terrible task, my children."

A new kind of shiver tightened Ruth's spine. Her arms twitched, as if to fold around her. Only with an effort did she straighten them.

„You must become Sturmwölfe. Tonight is the night when you cease to be students, and become warriors."

He passed between them, moving at last to the mysterious long table. With gloved hands, he grasped the tarp and flipped it back, somehow arranging the fold so it fell with military crispness though the gesture seemed casual.

Ruth bit back a gasp. Six long poles lay on the table— spears, each tipped with a glittering steel blade like a beech leaf, four-edged and as long as her hand. The spears also each had a crossbar lashed a third of the way up the shaft and a wrapped leather grip at the butt.

Six. One for each student.

„Choose your weapons," Herr Professor said. „And then we will go and meet your enemy."

The spear was heavier than Ruth expected, the butt as thick as her wrist. She propped the shaft against her shoulder, as Herr Professor demonstrated, and steadied it with her left hand crossed over her chest. The rain had not abated. It soaked Ruth's hair, plastered her blouse to her girdle, and when they left the paved path, trooping like ducklings after Herr Professor, it wet the lawn so mud oozed through the grommets and the canvas walls of her tennis shoes and her feet slid against the rubber soles.

Now the war was over, you could get rubber again. If you were Prussian. Ruth vaguely remembered shoes with rubber soles and buggies with rubber tires from before the invasion, when she was small. But these were the first such she'd had as an adult.

She rather thought this expedition would be the ruin of them.

Ruth was nearly last in line, Adele beside her and Jessamyn Johnson, who rarely talked, alone at the back of the group because Katherine was walking first. So Adele was in perfect position to appreciate how surreal the scene had become—the young women in their sodden white physical education uniforms marching with kicked-up knees like soldiers, or like a corps of drum majorettes with enormously oversized, deadly batons.

Herr Professor led them down the garden path between tall yew hedges. Ruth's whole body shook with cold, water dripping from her eyelashes and flooding down the collar of her shirt. The spear trembled, the point swaying like a wind-tossed tree-tip, and she expected an ambush at any moment. From the taut stares the other students flashed to every side, Ruth thought she was not alone.

She had some warning when they rounded the corner beyond the brick garden house, because the girls before her stumbled and reacted, moving raggedly into a semi-circle rather than falling out crisply to either side as they should. When Ruth came up among them, she saw why and stumbled too.

Between two old stone hitching posts, a drenched and miserable yellow-eyed wolf cringed at the limit of its chains.

„You will kill it." Herr Professor's voice rose from the shadows at the base of the hedge as if from a bottomless hole. „And when you have killed it, you will cut out the heart, and share it between you. Miss Small, Miss Mapes, you may begin."

—⊸≋⊶—

If there was a thing you could say for Ian MacGregor, it was that he had the gift of timing. He appeared at Abby Irene's door in the company of a smiling, red-headed wampyr just as Mrs. Moyer was setting the table for a late and lavish tea of poached salmon and green peas with crème brûlée for dessert. Abby Irene invited him to dine, and the wampyr—Alice—to observe.

MacGregor wasn't any younger than she. Despite his cane and artificial foot, however, he was considerably more spry. And he accepted the invitation with alacrity, and without even glancing over her shoulder for Sebastien as if Sebastien were her keeper.

Which might have lessened the pain of the wampyr's acid beauty when she smiled so kindly at Abby Irene. But couldn't, really.

Abby Irene wouldn't mind dying, she thought. Not now, not after so many years of adventures.

But by God, she minded getting *old*.

It was Sebastien's practice to attend the meal for company, and the presence of Alice and Mr. MacGregor only encouraged that. Abby Irene had never minded discussing business over food, and Phoebe had the strongest stomach of all of them. So as soon as Mrs. Moyer disappeared into the kitchen to bring forth the soup tureen, Abby Irene gestured to their guests. "You wouldn't have come out in this rain if the news could have waited until morning."

"Lady Abigail Irene." He looked up from adjusting his napkin. "You should have been a detective."

She contemplated tossing her roll at him, but Phoebe disapproved of food fights. So instead she snorted—unladylike, but that was the privilege of age—and said, "Out with it, or I'll see you get no crème brûlée."

He grimaced, burled hands interwoven on the lace tablecloth, and glanced at Alice, who gestured him to continue with an elegant white hand. "It turns out our friends already have files on these children."

He didn't expect to surprise her with that. But his gaze flickered from her, to Phoebe, to Sebastien, observing reactions. "All the girls are seventh daughters," said Abby Irene. "Tell me I'm wrong."

MacGregor clucked. "Lady Abigail Irene, I would wager no man could dare proffer such an opinion."

The flattery curved the corner of her mouth into an irrepressible smile. "You know me well."

He swirled the water in his glass. "One of the girls is a Jew. Her family are ours."

Sebastien flexed his fingers against the tabletop. "And she hasn't given them up?"

"She hasn't."

Mrs. Moyer came to lift away their plates and carry them into the kitchen. As she brought back the crème brûlée, Sebastien said, "That's a very suggestive fact. Has anyone admitted that the child is an infiltrator?"

MacGregor shook his head.

Alice leaned forward on her forearms and said, "We have to assume that many of these children are beyond immediate rescue, you must understand. Possibly beyond redemption at all, but—" She interrupted herself with a shrug. "They're young. They're easily swayed by philosophies that seem to provide uncomplicated answers and a sense of identity. The Prussians selected them when they were eleven or twelve. So we must recall that they've been indoctrinated to the Prussian ideals for as long as they have been aware of politics. And the Prussian ideals—"

"Everyone likes to be told they are special, chosen," MacGregor said. Abigail Irene watched his face go still and impassive as a death mask. "Everybody likes to be invited into the secret society."

Ruth had to try it herself, if only to put the poor thing out of its suffering. After a few steps, the simple act of forcing her feet forward proved an impossibility. None of the other girls had managed to totter even a step. They clumped in a semicircle, spear-butts propped on the ground before them, huddled behind the shafts as if they were the trees of a forest that could manage to hide them.

But then Adele stepped forward, and Ruth had to step up with her. Jaw firm, eyes front, and in the rain who could tell if they were too bright? Side by side. For now, they could do anything together.

For now. Until Ruth had to decide who to betray, Adele or herself.

Ruth lifted her spear and thrust, and for the first time killed something other than a sandbag. Adele shouted and thrust also, simultaneous.

It wasn't easy or clean, not the way they were taught in drill. Oh, the spear blade parted the skin like glass, but the wolf did not simply fall down and die. There was a terrible noise and struggle, the wolf lunging to the end of its chain, its claws harrowing the earth in parallel furrows, clods and mud flung to spatter dresses and faces. Ruth tasted salty earth, mud, rain, the sharp chlorophyll of torn grass.

Then finally it fell, and Adele stood leaning on her spear, hair plastered across her bloody face, shuddering over the chained body of the wolf.

Because she could not put her arm around Adele, not with Herr Professor watching, Ruth knelt down on the soaked grass beside the corpse and reached up without looking for the knife he would press into her hand.

So I can kill something if I have to, Ruth thought. *That's good to know.*

A man will surely be easier than a wolf. Especially a man who isn't blameless.

Once Ruth punched through the hide, the knife was sharp enough to slice flesh without sawing. Ruth was a farm girl; she'd never slaughtered, but she'd cleaned chickens. This was awful, but not so different. Adele and Beatrice and Jane helped her, once she had the belly open, and they pulled free a steaming mass of offal and left it in the mud. Jane turned her head to retch; Adele pulled back hands held from her sides as if they were daubed with flour.

Herr Professor had to free the heart.

Wolves, Ruth thought with some amusement, weren't kosher. But then, she'd been eating treif for years, in this German household.

God would forgive her. And if he did not, there were worse things he would be holding her accountable for.

The meat was hot, the shreds still smoking and flavored with cold rain, a shock of jellying blood and salty muscle, the heart…the heart tasted…the heart, the strength of it thrilling in her veins like liquor, like love…like nothing she'd ever before known.

When she raised her face from the palmful of blood and haggled meat she's swallowed, Ruth saw Adele grinning at her through a mask of gore rain-streaked across her cheeks. Ruth wanted to shudder, to cringe from the bizarre delight that prickled like nettles along every limb and down each finger, to hide her own face from the wildness that infected Adele's.

You're doing it for your mother, Ruth told herself, but the reflection might have been on bedtime chores or cold toast for all it stirred her. She wiped rain and blood from her nose onto the back of her hand, and thought more firmly, *You are doing it for Adele.*

"The second formula is: *sium*, cowbane; *aconum vulgare*, sweet flag; *pentaphyllon*, cinquefoil; *vespertilioris sanguis*, bat's blood; *solanum somniferum*, deadly nightshade; and *oleum*, oil."

—Montague Summers, *The Werewolf in Lore and Legend*, 1933

When Sebastien came into Abby Irene's bedroom, he found her before the mirror, brushing out her short white cap of hair. Her nightgown spread over the embroidered cushion of her vanity bench. She couldn't have seen his reflection float up behind her, but she still lifted her chin and the brush stilled.

He waited. If he were still flesh and blood, he would have held his breath. He felt, as he felt so often now, as if he were a burned paper, ashes still holding their shape but only so long as he remained untouched.

He placed a hand on the slope of her shoulder.

"Sebastien."

"My dear," he said. "You are afraid for me."

She snorted and set the silver-backed brush down on her vanity. "I am old," she said, scornfully. "My liver is weak. My heart is feeble. I have no stomach for risk and adventure any longer."

"You used to be a better liar," he said, tolerantly.

She pressed a powder-soft cheek against his hand. "Are you so certain I'm lying?"

"You have the heart and stomach of a general," he said. "And the liver of a king."

That straightened her neck and made her bark laughter. "I am too old to lose you, Sebastien. You are all I have left." She kept her eyes on the mirror, as if it were easier to speak to what she could not see. Her lips pressed tight, as if she understood the hypocrisy of proclaiming age and loneliness to a wampyr. She shook her head, a quick little shiver he might have mistaken for a tremor if she had not said, "By God, I'm a selfish old bitch."

"You're a selfish old bitch who's lucky to have chosen a wampyr lover." Hard words softened by an amused tone, and a kiss on the part of her hair. Her thin skin pressed warm to cold lips. "Abby Irene, I will not leave you."

"Don't promise that. You can't promise—"

"I have," he reminded, "demonstrated unrivalled reliability so far."

It made her laugh, which was his intention. But the laughter fell away again. She said, "I would have died for him if I could."

"For him?"

She shook her head like an old horse irritably shaking off a fly. "Don't play naive for my benefit, wampyr. Jack. And no, not for him. That's not what I mean, really. But I would have taken his place for you."

"Abby Irene—"

"Don't lie to me."

"*Don't.*" His tone, and whatever was in it—command, hurt, anger—at last made her turn and look at him, instead of the reflected emptiness where he was standing. "Don't pretend you know what I want or need, Abby Irene. Don't do it. Don't assume I am lying when I say I value you. I would not trade you for him."

"Or him for me?" But the bitterness had fallen out of her voice, and now she squinted at him without her glasses, eyebrows trying to rise. "I'm sorry, Sebastien. It's unbecoming. It's just the damned arthritis making me miserable. And you could have had so much *more* of him—"

He squeezed her shoulder. "Twenty years or eighty, what does it matter?"

"Sebastien?"

His turn for the edgy bitterness. "Really. Twenty years or eighty? What does it matter to me? You're all ephemera, woman. Gone before I know it, like your nations and your languages and your kings."

You didn't say such things to mortals. But Abby Irene stared at him for a moment, the squint surprised off her face, and then broke into a wide pink-gummed grin. "Bloody old bastard," she said. "Just when I was about to wade into my self-pity with both feet."

He grinned back, with enough teeth to make up for her lack of them. "Dance with me."

"As if I could."

"Stand on my shoes. I'll hold you up."

She blinked. "That's hardly dignified."

He slid his hand down her arm to the elbow, cupped it, and pulled her to her blue, horny feet. "And you were never sixteen, Abby Irene?"

She had shrunk. She tilted her head way back to look at him. "Not in living memory," she quipped, and let him bear her up, one hand at her waist, the other crossing her back as he lifted her to stand on his shoes. She weighed no more than the autumn-dry shell of a burst milkweed pod, blown clean by the wind. He helped her balance, careful to keep her weight off her knees, while she flung one arm around his neck and clung with an old woman's determination.

Carefully, in rhythm to the music she hummed under her breath, Sebastien stepped to the left. "I'm going to talk to them tonight," he said against her ear. "I'll get them out. We'll go like smoke. It will be all right."

"All of them?" She leaned back, supporting herself on hands crooked against his nape. "All twenty-one? What makes you think they'll come, especially the older ones?"

His mouth twisted. "It has to be all or nothing. We cannot allow the Germans to take them. If I can convince the older girls, remove the headmaster and the guards—"

Remove was a euphemism for permanence. But Abby Irene merely looked up at him, shaking her head so the soft skin under her throat wobbled. She had no pity for the Huns. Her concerns were of a far more mundane nature.

"Sebastien—" She leaned in to him, shifting her slight weight so he could support it more easily. "And how exactly do you propose to hide twenty-one children in occupied London when the whole of the Prussian forces will be turning the city upside down for them?"

"Do you propose I slaughter the lot?"

She shook her head. "That would be a last resort, and you know it. And an ineffective one. You know these can't be the only ones."

Of course not. It would be basest idiocy to think so. With their addiction to Nordic mysticism and the more bizarre fringes of eugenics—

"The Prussians," he said, "have a pattern. And they believe they are reclaiming their own and redressing ancient wrongs. How many blonde seventh daughters do you suppose there are in all the Aryan *Urheimat?*"

"Too many," Abby Irene said. "They must have such a school in every country in Europe. It would be very...Prussian...to standardize. Sebastien, we cannot allow the Prussians these soldiers. As long as Russia holds out there's a chance." It was bitter for her to speak supportively of England's old enemy, but a measure of her determination that she did so.

She continued, "If they have come to subscribe to the Prussian ideology—" She shrugged, but he could see it hurt her—her own expedience, and the cruelty of it. "Find me one. One we can make our own. You cannot save them, but perhaps we can *use* them."

"I think," Sebastien said, "I can find one or two who have not. I'll go tonight."

"Without an invitation?" She glared at him through her glasses. "How do you think to enter?"

"It's an old house," he said, noncommittal. "And I am an old fiend. I've been in London before. Let us not forget! Your are talking to Amédée Gosselin."

He hoped to make her laugh with his flourishes, but instead the hard squeeze of her hand on his arm arrested the dance. "Sebastien—"

She wanted to ask who had lived there, and when, and under what circumstances he had been invited in. The implications followed after, the realization that once intromitted, the devil could not be easily denied. Sebastien watched the tracks of thoughts chase one another across her face, shadowy and sharp, until she reined them back. Instead, she said, "An old house. How old?"

"When it was built, it stood in the countryside, surrounded by gracious lawns and manicured gardens. It's outlasted fire and plague," Sebastien said. His lips quirked. "And the Great Beer Flood of 1814."

"The Sorcerer's Fire?" Abby Irene asked. "It never got that far. There wasn't any *city* there at that time."

The Sorcerer's Fire was not so named so because sorcerers had begun it, but because the antecedents of Abby Irene's former colleagues—the Enchancery, at that time still tentatively and formally identified as the New Royal College of Sorcery—had been the only force in London capable of diverting the fire. That any of the hunched old medieval buildings of Central London—the coaching inns, churches, and slump-shouldered mushroom-cap houses huddled ear by ear, leaning heavily across narrow streets—still stood was due entirely to the courage of those grave men of history. Sebastien still remembered the horror and wonder that had swept the continent in its wake, and how quickly the kings of Sweden, Spain, and Portugal—among others—had rallied to follow the Germans and English in institutionalizing court magic and the training of sorcerers.

"And don't think you're going to distract me into history lessons," Abby Irene continued. "Do you think for an instant there won't be wards?"

He smiled and spun her, careful not to whirl too fast. "I don't think for an instant there will be wards that you can't bypass, my heart."

"It won't work," she said. "You will not persuade them."

"So you propose what? That I go in like a monster, and festoon the gate spikes with their heads?"

"No," she said. "Remember what I told you about the magic?" She reached into the collar of her gown, between her breasts, and pulled free a tiny chamois bag. She slipped the ribbon over her head and slid it into the breast pocket of Sebastien's coat, her crabbed old fingers lingering. "The one you choose. Give her this to drink in water. If she accepts the draught, that will serve us as consent."

"Spells of mesmerism, Abby Irene? That's quite unethical."

She closed her eyes, pressed a papery cheek to his shoulder. She whispered, "Time of war."

Hours dripped by, but even after a hot, necessary bath and a coat of stinking herbal liniment that stuck her flannel nightgown to her body, Ruth still felt the heart searing her belly. Cold-fire waves radiating from under her ribcage as if she had swallowed an ember—or ice—left her curled up and shivering, knees pressed against her mouth. She could not stop shaking. She pressed her thumbs under her chin to hold her teeth together because it was the only way to keep them from chattering. In the hall, she heard soft footsteps, but did not lift her head. Herr Professor had again instructed them to leave their bedroom doors open, and filtered light—from electric lamps turned low in the corridor—gave odd textures to the darkness in Ruth and Adele's bedroom.

It wasn't just Ruth's stomach that felt burned. Her skin prickled from scalp to toes, sunburn needles over every inch of skin. Across the gap between narrow beds, Ruth heard Adele breathing harshly, the pained whine seeping thinly between her teeth. She wasn't sleeping either.

And Ruth needed sleep so badly. If she could just sleep, just let go of the sickness and ache and burning in all her muscles, she thought she would be better. Desire became obsession, the need like a hag-riding, except awake rather than sleeping. Which was the problem, wasn't it? She should get up, cross the narrow space to Adele's bunk, and curl up beside her. She should pull Adele into her arms and comfort her.

But when Ruth pushed her fingers into her mouth she tasted the wolf's blood, the same blood that had smeared across Adele's face. She had scrubbed under the nails until the quicks bled too, and her own blood tasted like the wolf's blood. There was no difference between them.

It had been a game until now, spy against spy, Ruth playing secret agent and Ruth playing wolf-girl. The scents, the quickness. The way sound carried to her ear, as it had never carried before. The little magics that let her and Adele slip through the city on mischief, magics as real and as superficial as their uniforms. What burned through her now wasn't a game.

It was wildfire.

The dim light in the room dimmed further, in passing, as if somebody had briefly darkened the crack between door and jamb. Ruth waited until the shadow passed and the footsteps retreated down the hall before she lifted her head. She didn't whisper; whispers carry. Instead, she pitched her voice as low as possible and said, "Adele?"

Adele raised her face from her pillow and turned, her braid falling across her shoulder with a slide and thump so loud Ruth winced. *That* wasn't right. Or rather, it was right, because it made her realize in context that the heavy footsteps in the hall were someone padding softly by in slippered feet, and that the brittle rattle of rain on the shutters was in truth the fading patter of the passing storm. She could smell Adele across the gulf between their beds, the poison herbs in their bedtime liniment, the well-cured hide of the wolfskin belt sewn about her waist, as broad as the span of three fingers.

"Here," Adele murmured.

Ruth made herself untangle the tight knots of her body. She smoothed herself under the covers, rolled onto her back, and composed herself, hands across her breast. It was an artificial relaxation, but she could make herself stop shivering if she concentrated all her will on releasing the muscles, making them slack.

"I didn't think he could really do it," Ruth said.

"He?"

„Herr Professor."

„Make us like wolves." Adele's voice was firm, not rising. A confirmation rather than a question. „Do you think this is it? Will we go to Prussia now?"

She sounded half-excited, half-concerned. Ruth's heart ached. „Do you think they'll separate us?"

„Would they?" *That* chafing sound was Adele's calluses against skin as she rubbed her arms, not in chill but in self-comfort. „They wouldn't. They'll want us together. We're sworn to protect the Chancellor. What do you think they'll do with us?"

Ruth considered. She considered also the caustic river that scalded her limbs, the restlessness it bore with it. Moving felt better than lying still. Even if Herr Professor was doing bed checks. She rose to bare feet between the beds, spurning her slippers, and paced to and fro just at the length of Adele's reach. She knew it was the length because Adele extended one arm and let her fingertips brush and rebrush the skirt of Ruth's nightgown.

„The Prussians are strong," Adele said. „Maybe they're right. Why shouldn't they be right? Isn't God on their side?"

Might does not make right, Ruth wanted to say. *No matter how much it might seem like it sometimes.* But that would have been a stupid thing to say, just now. „Somebody's on their side," Ruth said grudgingly. „Are you?"

Adele shrugged. „They're smart and what they say makes sense. There's enough to eat. A good place to sleep. Everything is so much better than it was at home." The stretch of Ruth's own nightgown around each stride was deafening. Her head swum with the reek of herbs and rendered fat. Adele said, „There's you."

Ruth stopped mid-stride and turned into Adele's bed like a ship turning into the wind. „And you." She bent her fingers together. „Do you think we'll really be wolves?"

„No." Another serpentine rustle of Adele's braid upon the pillow. „We'll be warriors who are like wolves. Stronger, smarter. We'll go to Berlin. We'll go together. We'll be very brave in our uniforms and have the safest job in the army. We'll work hard and save pennies and buy a little townhouse, if they let us sleep outside the barracks."

Ruth closed her eyes. She could see it. A rose bush by the door, at the little table a pair of white-painted chairs. They could be like bachelor sisters, and nobody needed to know otherwise. „That would be sweet," she said.

She climbed back into bed to try to ride out the burning. Down the hall, clear as bells tolling, the footsteps receded still.

5.

IN THE NIGHT AND the rain, nothing could touch the wampyr. He was as at home in these savage elements as a statue: as obdurate, as immutable, as immune—to chill, to neglect, to solitude. But not to loneliness.

Oh, if only.

The boarding school—set amid its extensive garden— that hosted the operations of the Bund Englischer Mädel was well-enough known for God-fearing Englishman to avoid it. If Abby Irene had at first been reluctant to assist the wampyr, logic (he flattered himself)—or perhaps her knowledge that lacking her assistance would not stop the wampyr from attempting the rescue anyway—had swayed her. So he went with his wrists spiraled in copper wire, and copper coins in his shoes, spells of silence and stealth hung all about him.

Due to the weather and the distance of travel, the wampyr availed himself of the Tube, and emerged near

Tottenham Street in a gentler rain than had driven him underground. He'd caught the last train; as he stood on the street corner, umbrella cocked into the wind, he imagined it rumbling on towards its den for the night, like an asthmatic dragon.

For a moment, he stood listening to the rain, the way it swept in veils like the walls of a moving labyrinth. If he'd been human, he might have drawn breath or squared his shoulders, any of the small comforting gestures people performed to settle their resolve. Those had fallen away over the centuries, until only the wampyr was left behind, chill and still.

It didn't matter. His own gestures, if he even remembered them, would be the habits of a foreigner to modern eyes. In human company, he mimicked the mannerisms of those with whom he interacted, reflecting them like the mirrors that could not reflect him in turn.

He was a corpse.

The wampyr snorted at himself. *Almost by definition. Enough petulance, creature. Faint heart never won fair maiden.*

He turned along Tottenham Street, blown by the satin-cold wind. The walled grounds of the boarding school that had once been a country house occupied several acres, a snatch of parkland preserved in the center of a pseudopod of city stretched along Tottenham Court Road as if London groped blindly down a wire.

The wampyr passed a spiked gate flanked by gas lamps, hunkered under his umbrella as if he had not noticed the break in the fourteen-foot wall. A chill wind blew through the grille, still adorned with the wrought-iron monogram of the family who had dwelt there before the conquest. The scent of blood wound heavy through the rain, sharpening the wampyr's senses. The blood was not human.

He kept his stride even, unhurried, a professional man walking home late, and did not lift his head to breathe deep and savor. In the darkness beyond the mantle of the lamps, he leaned against the wall, umbrella cocked at an awkward angle and one foot lifted as if he had kicked a stone into his shoe. He held himself still as only a wampyr could, straining into the darkness, and heard feet on patrol inside the wall. Two sets, light and quick, and the smell of freshly-bathed young women overlaid by the blood he'd noticed before. Wolf-blood, and the girls themselves smelled musky, musty, as if a patina of tarnish overlaid the sweetness of their skin. They smelled of bitter herbs and rendered fat, even more so than they smelled of themselves.

The wampyr made sure he stayed upwind.

When the patrol had passed, the wampyr turned his attention to the wall. Fourteen feet, of dull gray granite repaired here and there over the centuries with patchy mismatched brick, the mortar along the top studded with broken glass. An amendment of the Industrial age, that last.

To the wampyr, an obstacle unworthy of consideration. He closed his umbrella with a rattle and lay it in the shadows along the bottom of the wall. His gloves in his pocket, he laid cold hands on cold stone and lifted himself off the ground.

He was light and dry and strong, and so he hunkered atop the wall in instants, balancing on flexed toes among the knives of glass. From here, he could see perfectly—through the dark—the two women in white (a ridiculous affectation, even for Prussians, whom the wampyr found consistently preposterous) their backs bisected by the black outlines of machine guns.

Glass sliced bloodless flesh when the wampyr let himself drop lightly inside of the wall. The wound sealed instantly, before the earth even dented under his shoes. He crouched into the shadow of a rain-huddled yew as one of the girls turned, scanning the wall with a frown.

Good ears. He waited until she'd shaken her head and turned away before he rose from his shadowed corner and slunk forward along the wall. There were dogs; he could hear them in the runs, and at least two loose in the gardens. But he was less worried about dogs than about the patrolling Ulfhethinn. And they were Ulfhethinn, if they were not lycanthropes—or both. It would be senseless to deny it now.

The smell of blood was stronger here, and he was walking towards the source. That wasn't the scent he needed to follow, though, and the girls on patrol weren't the ones he needed to talk to first. The rain intensified scents, both those of the girls he hunted and those of everything that could distract him from them.

The young women he had followed and protected shared a bedroom, which the wampyr found unsurprising. He paused below it, beside the grape arbor and the climbing roses, and craned his neck back so the rain fell on his face. Bad options, both—too much noise, and too much chance of leaving evidence behind. And if he did, there was probably a Zaubererdetektiv somewhere in London that could link it back to him.

And that would not be very much like either Amédée Gosselin *or* the Scarlet Pimpernel. As well as dangerous to his court. No, he would climb the brick. The room he needed was on the second story anyway, and not too long a climb.

He surmounted it with ease, brick-grit enough purchase to defeat the slipperiness from rain, and—counting on the cat-curiosity of teenaged girls—scratched at shutters barred against the storm.

Movement answered within. The wampyr dropped below the edge of the casement as the bar was slipped, only to rise again after the shutters swung wide. A girl leaned out. Her icy-pale hair, braided for bed, fell forward over her shoulders and was instantly jeweled with raindrops. "Rapunzel, Rapunzel," the wampyr said, clinging to the window-ledge, from so close that he would have had only to turn her face to kiss her.

He expected her to recoil, but she didn't—neither like a startled child, nor like a threatened wild thing. Rather, she turned deliberately enough to convince the wampyr that she had been aware of his presence all along. She met his gaze unblinking. "You," she whispered. "Doctor Chaisty."

He shouldn't have been surprised, but he'd let her have the advantage. "You know me?"

"From the street," she said. "You protected us. You smell different, you know." She glanced over her shoulder, into the dark room behind. "This isn't safe. They made us sleep with the door open. And Adele—"

"I shall come in," the wampyr said, and with an easy swing brought himself through the window and onto the floor beside her. The old warped floorboards, rough and splintery, did not even creak under his weight as he crossed the felted rug in the center of the room and placed himself in the corner behind the door. The blonde hurried to him, her footsteps nearly as silent, fearless as she backed him into the corner. "Adele is *sleeping*—"

"Then be soft," the wampyr said, too low for human ears to hear. From the movement of the young woman's eyes, he knew she suffered no failure in understanding. "And we shall not wake her. Are you Ruth?"

Surprised, she nodded. The surprise falling away, she said, "You heard us, too."

"I know Adele is happier here than you."

She stood back, allowing him the freedom of the room.

He considered her. It was a contemporary conceit, time spent alone, sleeping single in a bed. A modern luxury made possible by coal fires and inexpensive, machine-woven bedding. The wampyr found privacy a convenience, but centuries of experience had proven that it was hardly a necessity. Even while dealing with Ulfhethinn? Well, it would be an interesting challenge, in any case.

And if he failed, that would be interesting, too. The wampyr was too old to believe in the sanctity of human governments or human religions. He'd seen too many rise and fall, too many fragile, ephemeral men and women give everything to support or oppose them. He did believe in justice, and in the greatness of the human spirit, and in the correctness of a human desire to live in relative safety, comfort, and freedom. But Abby Irene was still young, as the Blood reckoned the centuries—"fourscore is but a girl's age," Christopher Marlowe had written, when he had barely a score himself—and her England, and her King in exile still mattered to her. And Abby Irene—mattered to the wampyr.

The older he got, the simpler the world was revealed to be.

The girl said, "You're not human, are you?"

The wampyr smiled. Even in the dark, he knew she saw it, as well as might one of his own Blood. He could tell by the way she licked her lips and dropped her eyes. "As human as you," he said. "Which is to say, I was born it."

She stared at him, as if considering that took all her concentration. And then she nodded curtly.

"Then come with me. Herr Professor has gone to bed, Can you hear him snoring?"

The wampyr could, two floors below, if he listened very, very carefully over the warm-air grate by the door. The girl, from her smile, heard him plainly, and was amused at the evidence of how superior her senses were to the wampyr's. "Herr Professor," she said, "thinks he knows how to deal with us. But he does not really." She widened the gap of the door with her fingertips. Her eyes shone in the reflected light like any predator's. "We can talk in the library. The books soak up sound."

The library was just across the hall, and its door was shut tight, only darkness showing underneath. Still, the girl paused beside it, tilted her head, and breathed deep. The wampyr mimicked her; the room beyond, insofar as his nose could tell him, stood empty. The girl licked her lips, glanced over her shoulder, and turned the handle with such exquisite slowness that the vampire did not even hear the click of the latch. She ushered him inside, into a hushed cold space that smelled of leather and camphor and the residue of pipe-tobacco. Thick carpets dented almost imperceptibly under cat-light footsteps and Ruth shut the door behind them. Then she came to him, surefooted in nearly unrelieved dark, and paused less than a yard away.

She said, "What's your name? It's not really Chaisty, is it?"

"I am too old for names," he answered. "But you are young. You probably still remember yours."

"I also know better than to give it to monsters," she answered—just the shape of words on her lips, a sound so low even the wampyr could have convinced himself he imagined it.

He let his smile widen. He admired self-determination. He said, "Ruth Grell."

Her surprise could not be feigned, not with the way it came with the scent of sweat on her skin, the acceleration of her pulse in the soft places of her neck. "How did you learn that? You didn't overhear it all in the alley."

The wampyr leaned forward. What he had to say, he wouldn't say out loud, even so softly no one but Ruth might learn its rhythms. "Your family is Jewish," he murmured against her ear. "And of German descent. You have lost loved ones to the Prussians and their extermination camps."

She folded her arms across the white overlapped lapels of her dressing-gown and said, "Since you have no name of your own, perhaps I shall call you Dracula."

Bravado would do; sometimes it matured into courage, and if not, sometimes it could take the place. He said, "We know why you are here, Ruth. You are an infiltrator. At first we thought to intervene, to rescue you and the other girls."

"I won't leave," she said flatly. "I've come too far."

"We know," he said. "We realized this could not be the only such school, is it? Ruth, do you hate the Prussians? Are you going to turn your classmates against them? Because we can help."

He wasn't expecting her bitten lip, the turned-away face of suppressed laughter. "You don't know as much about what I'm doing here as you think. It's too late. We killed the wolf tonight, and we must swear an oath at dawn. To the Chancellor. A sorcerously *binding* oath. After that, they are going to send us to Berlin, where we will become the first of the Sturmwölfe."

She glanced back, eyes raised to study his face under flickering lashes. The sideways light from the door cast blurry shadows through them, making exhaustion-bruised eyes seem as if she had painted around their rims like an older woman. "The Chancellor's private guard," she said.

From her face, her tone, the way she angled her head, the wampyr understood that there was more. He waited, though, and watched her face, and eventually she wound her hands one around the other and said, "Adele believes in this. In the Prussian homeland. In the empire. She's not the only one."

"You?" he asked.

She opened her mouth to answer, caught herself, and said more carefully, "I am here because of what I believe in. And because the Chancellor requires my service, to keep the empire strong."

As if what she believed in and what the Chancellor required were separate things, to be separated by a long weighty pause.

The wampyr said, "What you believe in? It is not simply that where Adele goes, you go?"

Ruth chewed her lip. The wampyr would have put his arms around her if she were his, but when she looked up again he saw the cold yellow spark floating in blue irises like the killing sun in a noonday sky. No creature of the night, this wolf-maiden. Not the moon-touched shape-changer of painful experience. She was something else, and in the face of it, even the wampyr stepped back. He thought she might even be fiercer and more terrible than a lycanthrope, because there was no lack of awareness in her gaze, and lupine cunning had not replaced human intellect—but supplemented it. She said, "It has nothing to do with Adele."

The wampyr fought a rising chill, and kept his frown from his face as much as possible. "And if we offered to extract you?"

"None of the girls will go with you willingly."

"We can protect them. We can protect their families. Young King Phillip has been welcomed in his exile by the government of the Americas, and we have the means to extract all of you from England and make you safe. You would be welcomed in the fight against the Prussians, you know."

"I am in the fight against the Prussians," she hissed.

He blinked. And wondered how he could have been so blind. *The Chancellor's private guard,* she'd said.

Ruth turned away. Her crossed arms crept higher, tighter against her chest. "You'd better go."

"Ruth—"

"Devil," she said. "Do not tempt me. You can make us safe. Very well. Do you think we're the only ones? Do you think the Chancellor will fail to campaign against Russia, when he has consolidated his hold on Europe? When he has Russia, will he be content? Or will he find other uses for his Ulfhethinn, wampyr?"

When she stared at him, it was clear she expected him to look down. She could not know how little shame he still had in him, or how little investment in nationalism. "It seems," he said, "unlikely."

She nodded. "I also think not." She was so young, a child in a nightgown and robe, who should have been clutching a lop-eared velvet rabbit. But as she raised her chin in the darkness, her youth made no difference to the terrible sternness of her face.

Children. It was always children who believed so deeply, who risked so much.

Was it futile, the wampyr wondered? Or were they necessary after all? When he'd first glimpsed her, he'd thought she was like Phoebe, with her pale hair and careful demeanor. It proved that appearances meant nothing, yet again.

"Your oath to the Chancellor?" the wampyr asked.

"Oaths under duress…."

"A blood Wyrd? Your death to break it?"

"I have sworn a prior oath. Maimonides spoke of the immutability of the Torah as God's law. I became bat mitzvah at twelve. Before I came to this…school." Her lips curved in the dark. "My tribe before myself, wampyr. What's death to those stakes? And if I should somehow live long enough to need forgiveness, my religion provides for a day of atonement."

"How many in your class do you think will be assigned directly to the Chancellor?" That's what it would take, if assassination was what she intended.

She shrugged. "I shall have to excel. I am already among the best in my class. And *that* is why I cannot leave, your namelessness."

Children. Warriors. Of course her family knew, and approved. It was a choice of desperation. The wampyr said, "Even if you succeed—"

"I know."

Just as Jack would have spoken it.

Unmoving, the wampyr said, "What can I do to help?"

Ruth swung her arms. "Help me impress the Chancellor."

The wampyr reached into his breast pocket. He pinched the soft small pouch between his fingers and pulled it out. "Take this."

She did, without hesitation, and weighed it in her hand. "What is it?"

"A potion," he said. "It may change your lover's mind, if she will take a drink from your hand."

Ruth's eyes widened. Her fingers twitched, as if her hand wanted to close around the bag, and then a moment later her fist clenched on it.

"Oh," she said. She swallowed. "Thank you."

—⊗—

When Ruth came back to bed, alone, Adele was sitting up in the darkness. „I dreamed someone was in the room."

„I went to the library," Ruth answered, and leaned over to kiss Adele's forehead between her brows.

When Ruth leaned back, Adele raised her eyes. „Your hair is wet."

„I leaned out the window," Ruth said, hoping no one would find the damn carpets in the library before morning. Chances were good; there wouldn't be much time for reading before the ceremony. „Where it was cold. Your sheets are soaked with sweat. We should change them before you catch your death."

„That explains the puddles on the floor, then." Adele drew her knees up and wrapped her arms around them.

Ruth walked to the armoire, so Adele would not be able to see her face. She opened the doors, and while her back was turned, she slipped the pouch into her underthings. She could ask Adele right now if she wanted a cup of water—

Was she that unworthy of Adele's love? Would she resort to—not love spells. Brain-washing. Exactly like a Prussian?

Even to save Adele's soul and maybe keep her alive? Certainly, to keep her love.

Ruth brought down clean sheets, dusting aside lavender sachets that raised a scent of old ladies. „Come on," she said.

„Strip the bed. We need some sleep; we have to go to St Paul's in the morning."

Abby Irene raised her head from the crossword puzzle in the *Times* of London when Sebastien entered the living room. It was still two hours before dawn—not that you could tell without a glance at the clock, because clouds still sealed the sky like a lid—and he was wet to the skin.

"Is Jason awake? I need a message taken."

"I don't think so. But the bell would wake him."

Sebastien crossed the room to the pull, unspeaking.

Abby Irene said, "Your potential rescues?"

She knew the answer by how his lips pressed thin. But he shook it off—along with the rain from the shoulders of his black caped overcoat—and sat down across the table.

"Your plan," Sebastien said. "The Jewish girl had already adopted it."

"I beg your pardon?"

His smile split his face like a knife. "She means to assassinate the Chancellor. And Alice and I am to assist her in wining his confidence. So, my darling," he said, and she believed him. "Somewhere in that enormous library of yours, is there a plate of the nave of St Paul's?"

Judiciously, she folded the crossword and set it aside. "In fact, I think I can do better than that. When we moved the library in, I'm pretty sure I catalogued a folio of architect's plans and drawings of the great cathedrals of Europe. Do you suppose St Paul's is still a great cathedral of Europe, in this benighted age?"

6.

THE GREAT GOTHIC CATHEDRAL of St Paul's was longer than Canterbury Cathedral by some forty-five feet—585 feet long through the portico, nave, and choir—with a spire more than twice as tall. It loomed over the skyline of central London as it had since the wampyr first viewed that cramped medieval city. The centuries had altered its facade, its spire, and the architecture of its towers and approaches, but the essential church was the same.

The fourth Christian church on Ludgate Hill, it was begun by Normans in 1087 in the wake of a fire that destroyed much of London. Some of its blocks were salvage—from the earlier, smaller Saxon cathedral whose footprints it obliterated; from the Palatine Tower of the Conqueror, also lost in the conflagration—and there were places in the oldest parts of the church where you could still see black carbon on the stones. It had taken over two hundred years in the building, having burned again—incomplete—in the

London fires of the 1130s, though it had been spared the fire of 1212. The cathedral was consecrated and reconsecrated in 1240 and 1300, even before the completion of final construction in 1314. Since then, it had survived political upheaval, the stripping of its fixtures for gold or expediency, use as a stable, lightning—the hand of God demolishing one of the tallest spires in Europe at the height of the English Renaissance—a bizarrely classical western facade added by Inigo Jones, the Sorcerer's Fire, Christopher Wren's Baroque additions, 18th century restoration of the central tower to a wedding-cake standard, and the bombs rained from Prussian zeppelins and flying dreadnaughts.

If the cathedral had been built to the glory of God, well. God had not made the building of it easy.

The wampyr had years on this eight-hundred-and-fifty-one-year-old church, but only a century or two. Of all the products of artifice in Europe, he felt most kinship to cathedrals.

They grew and crumbled and endured through fat times and lean. They fell prey to fashion, to famine, and also to the whims of kings. Architects restored—or defaced—them. Conquerors appropriated them.

They endured war and revolution and the rare idylls between—but the essential outline never changed. The nave and choir and transept and crossing. The tower at the heart. The crypts beneath. The flying buttresses, transferring the thrust of the fan vaults to the foundations.

They were not living things, but they mocked living things. And in outlasting them, were changed by them, and became the rememberers of history.

St Paul's Cathedral housed the tombs of Aethelred the Unready, John of Gaunt, and John Donne. It seemed only fitting that the Prussians, with their fascination for appropriating myths and histories—and offspring—should consecrate their wolf-children there.

The wampyr came to St Paul's before even an ecclesiastical rising-time, traveling along in darkness and the cold continuing rain. Whatever legendry made of his kind, he had no allergy to holy ground. Though a church was the house of God, God did not see fit to demand the wampyr respect it as a dwelling. And so he made his way within.

Truly, the gates of heaven stood wide to any who would enter.

Paul's Walk, they called the mighty nave, for its length and the height of the vaulting. Now it clung with shadows, only the rainy light of the city beyond casting shimmers across the clerestory windows that could not penetrate them to illuminate the space within. That did not matter to the wampyr; the darkness was transparent to him. For a moment he paused to consider the echoing belly of the cathedral, said by some to have no rival for beauty among the medieval churches of Europe.

The wampyr, who had seen the cathedrals of Santiago de Compostela and Notre-Dame de Reims both in their youth and in their age, found the comparison overstated. Still, he wished he could have observed the windows in sunlight. Another sight he had never witnessed in all his long existence, and one of the ones he most regretted. He was of an age with the art of the stained glass window, and he had not seen its first incarnations when he was a mortal man.

This cathedral bore more resemblance to Reims or Canterbury than the famous Galician cathedral, which was of an older, barrel- and groin-vaulted design. Here in London, rib-vaults bore the weight of stone, overhead. The original lead-sheathed wooden roof was long since replaced, which had helped the great structure survive the fires of London and Prussian incendiaries as well.

A medieval cathedral had a different sense to it than a Renaissance—the wampyr stopped himself before he could think *modern*—one. Fan-vaults, the Renaissance standard, gave a sense that the stone was levitating, as if its weight had somehow been placed in abeyance for a time. Or as if it had, by some magic, been made weightless. As if granite and slate could fly.

In a nave such as this, however...*all* one felt was the heft of the rock suspended overhead, the thrust through the vaults and into the buttresses and walls, the stress and mass and pressure. The sheer massy bulk of it, and the muscle and wit it had taken to engineer those walls, that roof, those vaults and pillars.

For the glory of God, of a certainty. But when confronted with a cathedral, the wampyr found himself always marveling instead at the ingenuity and will of tiny, fragile men, to so overcome the hard obdurate laws of God's creation.

He would have liked to pad the length of that chill silent corridor, for symbolism's sake, but he had not grown to be older than churches by foolishness. Or at least, he allowed with an element of self-amusement, not by too much foolishness.

He ascended to the lovely Norman triforium, which would bring him the length of the nave in relative privacy. At the crossing, he paused, with Abby Irene's plan of the cathedral sharp before his mind's eye. There seemed no doubt that the oath would take place before the altar.

He made himself comfortable in the shadows, there to bide the hours until dawn. Another fine thing about England; he could be fairly sure the rain would hold.

An hour before sunrise, a figure appeared beside him, silent as a ghost, slender in her black opera cloak and gloves. When she looked up at him, he saw he top part of her face obscured by a black domino mask and smiled. "Alice," he whispered. "So glad you've come."

She winked, her eyelid pale in the almond-shaped aperture, and extended a hand. From it dangled a second black domino. "I thought we should match."

Ruth would have wakened Adele with a kiss, but when Herr Professor's footsteps again made the old wood of the corridors creak, the door to their room was still standing open. Behind their own doors, Ruth could hear the other girls stirring.

So Ruth merely rose, slid her feet into her slippers, and pulled her dressing gown from the head of the bed. She lit the gas lamps over the bed-heads. Then with deliberate motions she squared the sheet-corners and made her bed up taut, as if she would ever be returning to it. She was tucking the top sheet under fluffed pillows when a heavy tread along the hall runner alerted her, long before Herr Professor's knuckles sounded sharp on the doorframe. „Rise and shine," he barked, though Adele was already swinging her feet over the edge of her mattress. Who could sleep through all that tromping?

„Good morning, Herr Professor," Ruth said, Adele mumbling the formula along with her. Ruth's bed finished, she turned to help Adele pull her own sheets taut.

While Adele scrubbed in the washbasin, Ruth laid out pressed blouses, stockings, the shoes they had polished the previous day. Adele brought their ironed uniforms from the wardrobe and laid them on the bed beside the blouses. Ruth hid the soft tan leather pouch inside her palm, hoping her own scent would conceal its very faint one.

Hands emptied, Adele glanced at the door, touched Ruth's shoulder, and leaned forward. Ruth, expecting a furtive kiss, turned into the embrace, but Adele's mouth came inside the camber of her braid, instead, pressed close to her ear. „You're going to take the oath, right?"

Her eyebrows were drawn tight over the bridge of her little-girl nose. Ruth's mouth parched. She could not look down, because if she looked down, Adele would know she wasn't telling the truth. A rose bush by the door, a pair of white-painted chairs.

The pouch in her sweating palm.

We could live together. We could be safe and happy and privileged. Sturmwölfe.

Are the Prussians any worse than any other conqueror?

She thought of the Jews who hadn't been able to pass.

She thought of her own family.

They were bad enough, she decided.

„I'm going to take the oath," she said. „Pass me my hairbrush, Adele."

When Ruth and Adele trooped outside with the other girls, the long drive was lined not only with the usual bus, but with a half-dozen staff cars. Ruth began to walk toward the long gray bus, only to feel Herr Professor come up beside her. She felt him begin to reach for her shoulder, but he stopped himself, and let his hand fall to his side. „That is for the younger girls," he said. „The graduates ride in cars this morning."

She frowned at him, surprised. He smiled. He carried no umbrella, and the rain dripped from the brim of his uniform cap. Not the gray school uniform, tonight, but the polished black of the secret police, with the snarling wolf's-head on its shoulder. They weren't supposed to know that Herr Professor was also Colonel, but of course all the girls had whispered it behind their hands. And now, to see him so dressed—

„You will be officers in an hour," he said. He touched the wolf head. „You must be accorded dignity as officers."

For the first time in her memory, she saw him smile. He had a good smile, warming his plain rugged face, and an expectant expression. When she looked down, she saw his hand extended, for a formal clasp.

Hesitant, she took it.

„Congratulations, Miss Grell," he said, and gave her a squeeze that creaked his leather gloves. „Welcome to a glorious service."

The rain dripping down the clerestory windows across the nave, one level above the triforium, resolved into transparent streaks as gray light grew behind. Although the clouds would protect him from direct sun—as long as they held—the wampyr was careful to keep to the shadows. As much visual impact as he might have, leaping from above the arcade in flames, it was an experience he could as soon do without.

Alice skulked beside him, the cloak drawn close about her shoulders so she vanished into the shadows of the pillars.

She settled into herself, silent as the grave, breathless as a corpse, and made herself vanish.

She was growing up.

Ruth had said the cadets would arrive with the dawn the gray light heralded, so the wampyr was unsurprised when he heard footsteps below. Many footsteps, purposeful, and following them a swell of light.

The interior of the cathedral had been fitted with electric lights, many-branched chandeliers on their creaking chains. Alice drifted behind him like a ghost, at the ready. "Crypt," he murmured, and she departed as if the wind from the opening door had guttered her out.

As the wampyr peered through a pierced-stone grille that must have been worked by a master stonemason, he saw women enter the church and set about the homely tasks of keeping the house of the Lord. They brought green boughs and hothouse flowers for the altar, spread pressed linens so the crisp smells of sizing and lavender-water rose into the air. They brought bread and wine, set candles, laid out the liturgical tools. Before they were quite finished, just as they were squaring corners and effacing themselves, more busy footsteps joined them. The wampyr saw robed men moving briskly below, the military-tailored black-and-silver cassocks of German Christian clergy swinging from their shoulders. Among them, moving to the altar, was one whose black was relieved by masses of bullion, his white surplice flashing with crimson and gold embroidery and swinging tassels.

A Bishop of the German Christian church, then—a high Christian magician in service to the Chancellor. Someone who might have rivals, but few betters among the ritualists of the Church.

Abby Irene, Sebastien thought, would have to have been restrained from spitting over the rail. If she could have kept herself from laughing savagely at the irony of a pagan ceremony freighted with Christian pomp. Of course, it was all pagan at the root, was it not? Layers and layers and layers of time, things changed under their weight until they became almost unrecognizable. Like the wampyr, like the cathedral itself.

The flurry of activity took only three-quarters of an hour. The wampyr wondered if the organist would attend, but no crashing, experimental chords told of his arrival. The wampyr would have felt the bass notes as a rumble under his breastbone he thought would make a human heart stutter. It was just as well; he pitied the wolf-girls the delicacy of their ears. There was something to be said for the hearing of the dead.

There was no sign of choristers either, and the lack of music gave the assembly a furtive air. The great portico doors swung open, washing the warm yellow glow of electric light watery and gray. Now a larger group approached, though not by any means enough to make the cavernous interior space of the cathedral seem less vast and empty. Rather, the way they huddled together—a score of girls and young women in their cadet uniforms walking with every appearance of calm decorum up the center aisle until all but six of them filed silently into the pews on either side—made the weight of that enormous vault seem all the more oppressive.

The wampyr would have known which of the cadets was Ruth, even if he did not know her by her hair and scent. She was the one who resolutely kept her eyes level rather than gazing up in wonder at the interior heights of the spire as the cadets took their places in a double line before the altar.

The oath was long and complicated, punctuated with a number of pauses for thaumaturgy and call and response. *Surely,* Ruth thought, *fifteen minutes of swearing your life away was enough for anyone.*

She could not smell the wampyr in the cathedral, but she hoped that was because of the smell of lavender and human bodies and blazing candles and frankincense, and any care he might have taken to conceal himself, and not because he had not come.

She could still do it without him. She had always planned to go it alone. But one sharp distinguishment would make all the difference in her first assignment.

She could end it faster with his aid. And the sooner she did to the Chancellor what needed to be done, the sooner the youngest cadets could return to their homes.

The first row of cadets were moving forward single file, to lay their hands on the Bible and receive their benedictions. Just as Jessamyn was about to put her hand down, Ruth drew in a breath—

The wampyr vaulted from the triforium, cloak flapping and his face obscured behind a crimson velvet domino, and while the other cadets were scattering or scrambling aside, Ruth lunged forward. "For England and the king!" he bellowed, a voice that rang dust from the chandeliers like the great organ's hum.

Ruth almost heard him laughing as Herr Professor cooly, mechanically, in his own turn opened fire. She heard the bark of another woman's gun, and saw the bullets tatter the wampyr's cloak and do him no real harm. Ruth's revolver would not help her.

Something rose in her, sharp and vicious, a wildfire, a taste like metal on her tongue. The belt at her waist constricted, each of seven iron nail-heads cold-ice-hot against her skin. The wolf who had been Ruth leaped forward, cleared the altar steps in a bound, snatched up a silver-gilt candlestick and swung it like a mace. She did not want him dead, she remembered, and at the last instant pulled the blow somehow.

It was hard.

The wampyr raised his arm to block; she felt bone shatter. It discommoded him no more than the bullets. She heard her own snarl, a wolf-rising cry, and swung again—

for the face this time. Wolf, wolf. A new thing. An old thing made new—

Someone beside her, someone now with a broken staff in her hand. A spear, improvised.

Adele, of course it would be Adele, who had killed the wolf with her, who someday Ruth might have to kill herself.

But not today, she thought, and moved forward with her spear-sister to destroy the intruder. He tore up a pew— the younger girls had scattered, screaming, to a corner of the nave, and now Herr Professor placed himself between them and the intruder, while the Bishop scrambled back off the altar, clutching his pectoral—and hurled it. Ruth met the thing in the air, clutched it in outreached hands and flipped it up and over, end over end, to splinter against the pillars of the far arcade. She touched down toe-tip, Adele beside her, and then the coward swung around a pillar and fled.

What's the matter? The pack too fierce?

He fled like a darting hare, cover to cover. Though she and her sister slavered at his heels, the others racing behind, she could not quite catch him, even when she strained, snapping at his heels, Adele beside her. When he plunged down the stairs to the crypt she exulted—now I have you!—but then remembered.

She must not catch him. He was here for her. She must—

But she did not know how to lose him, with Adele beside her. She had no choice; she must give it her best effort, and run him to ground.

And with the lust for blood in her teeth, it would be easy. Easier to kill than to stop. Easier to rend than to protect. It was dim and red behind her, what she had intended. *Kill him. Kill the enemy.*

…except the dim whisper of reason would not let her. She thought she heard her Zayde's voice in her ear. She turned and snapped, as if at a clutching hand, and saw Adele shy in confusion behind her. And then the flap of cloaks, two now, wait—they darted like schooling fish and when she lunged for one, the other was there, cutting across her path. She lunged again, grabbed with one hand, swung her improvised mace. Adele jabbed with the broken pole; there was a flash of hair like fire as the wampyr's hood tore off. And then she—it was a she, behind the mask, and she was laughing—ducked aside and the first one was there before them again, so Ruth pivoted and leaped for him—

And something hit her in the ribs, hit her hard and knocked her sprawling. She rolled into shadows, gasping, her breath struck away, and pushed herself up on her elbows to chase a flickering shadow that smelled of cold and—very faintly, as if from long ago—cologne.

But he turned there by the gap between pillars, pressed a fingertip to his mouth—*shhh*—and mouthed *Godspeed* at her.

She checked herself. *Do not kill.* Though the wolf slavered in her. Do not kill.

She had promised her Zayde something. She would remember it.

Old oaths superseded new. She would remember who she was. She gritted her teeth, closed her eyes, determined. When she opened them again, Adele crouched beside her, sniffing heavily, the shattered pole in her hands slick with some dark substance. It did not—exactly—smell like blood.

Ruth put a hand on her haunch. Adele glanced over, panting like a train, the gold in her eyes dimming now.

„Damn," she said. „I think they're gone."

Abby Irene was there to meet Sebastien when he staggered into the hall. He leaned heavily upon the redheaded wampyr's shoulder, a handful of tattered black cloth wadded in his hand and pressed against his side. Abby Irene wheeled her chair forward, shouting for Jason and Phoebe and Mrs. Moyer, but Sebastien raised a and to keep her back.

"Uncomfortable close to a staking," he said. "Give me a little time to recover."

She stopped, and rolled her chair back. She was not afraid of him, or what he might do in his blood-lust, while injured. His control was a thing of legend—and in her weariness, she could have thought of no better way to die than feeding him. She was old; let her do something useful again.

Except it would break Sebastien's heart, whatever lies he told himself about her, and she knew that.

Abby Irene looked at the damned red-headed wampyr with her smooth translucent skin, her clear eyes, her strength to bear Sebastien up as if he weighed nothing at all. Abby Irene opened her mouth to order the wampyr to bring Sebastien inside, and the words caught in her throat.

For the first time in her life, she envied a wampyr.

And then she shook her head. *Soon,* she promised herself. *As soon as there is a King Phillip in England once more. You can let go then.*

She already heard feet on the stairs, but it didn't matter. Raising her voice again, she yelled, "Damn you, Phoebe, put on your slippers! Where are you?!"

She blinked stinging eyes behind the thick lenses of her glasses, and looked the deathless creature who was Alice Marjorie for now in the eyes. "Bring him into the parlor," she said. "We'll lay him down on the divan."

The wampyr followed her orders, as if there had never been any question at all.

Lieutenant Grell, her black wool uniform spotless from white blouse collar to spit-polished boots, disembarked the train in Berlin. She had expected Lieutenant Kneeland to meet her at the station, but while a crisp glance from one end of the platform showed many uniforms moving with brisk direction, none of them embraced the lean form of a Sturmwölf.

Someone said in her ear, „She had car trouble."

It was a dark-haired man of slightly more than medium height, slender, eyes shaded from the harsh glare of electric lights under a rakish bowler hat. He smiled, just a little, when he saw her.

Her nostrils flared on the cold, distant scent of undeath.

„Nothing serious?" Her palms should not sweat so. She was his equal, in strength if not in age.

The smile broadened. „Just a few loose wires. She'll no doubt be along before you have time to find a cup of coffee."

„So you met me at the station. How kind. That must have been hard traveling."

He winked, and quipped „*Denn die Todten reiten schnell.*"

She laughed. „Fast indeed. Did you have yourself shipped? Well, Count, I know you did not seek me out only for conversation—"

„I came," he said, „to give you a last chance to change your mind. And join your mother in New Amsterdam."

„And leave all this?" A bitter sweep of her gloved hand took in the garishly-lit station, the bustle of soldiers. „Not to mention Adele—"

„You did not give her the powder?"

Lip-biting, Ruth shook her head. She had not thrown it away, either, though she had meant to toss it from the train. She groped it from her pocket and thrust it at the wampyr, whose hands stayed stubbornly by his sides.

„Take it."

He tucked his hands behind his back. „Adele will not forgive you."

Lieutenant Grell nodded. „I'm not going to brainwash her."

„The Prussians already have. You lose her either way, you know. And this way, perhaps you lose your life as well." But he put his palm out and let her lay the pouch across it.

Ruth said, „So I will enjoy what I have, while I have it. Thank you for your offer. But no. I have my orders." She patted her pocket to make them crinkle. But those were not really the orders she meant.

He stepped back. „Failing that, I came to give you a name," he said, quietly. „A name you can find me under. Come and find me when the war is over. And you are alone. If you live, Ruth Grell."

It stopped her, that certainty. She raised her eyes to his. Where his hand had closed around the pouch, she brushed the back of his glove with the back of her own.

She swallowed. "If I live," she said in English. "I will."

She believed she was lying. But he thought she would be surprised, when everything was ended, when she had lost her Adele. She would be surprised to discover she had told him the truth, after all.